In Order of Appearance:

William Lafayette Snow, owner
of the hotel, and his wife, Helen
Their son, Will
Calvin Keats, the banker man
Frederick Lafayette Snow, brother
And dad
Children: Marilyn and P.J.
(also known as Junior Snow.)
Amm and Zasu, their protectors
Harry and Deane Dunne, chums
Neely, Grand Theatre manager

And don't forget the cook, Ms. Bertha,
And the Boxers.

THAT SNOW WOMAN

BY LOVEY SMITHAM

THAT SNOW WOMAN
ISBN: 9798511677521
COPYRIGHT: 7-16-2021
Lovey Smitham
All rights reserved

This is a book of fiction.
When products, people,
places or things are mentioned,
by name, copyright is neither claimed,
implied nor intended.

Also by Lovey Smitham:

2018
Old Sins Have Long Shadows
Madame's Grand Premiere & Sideshow
Dough, Ray & Me
2019
Rose Side Park
Ten Lizzies
Ice Tongs, A Weapon of Choice
2020
The Haunting of Norman Gold
Old Sins Have Long Shadows, 2nd. Ed.
Roxy LeRose
Mrs. Antique's Place
2021
In My Rotogravure

And now:

THAT SNOW WOMAN

THAT SNOW WOMAN

By: Lovey Smitham

No one knows what Will Snow wanted to be when he grew up. Maybe a pharmacist, like his father, William, who traded that dream education and vocation to run his new Hotel Snow, in Grand Saline, Texas, thirty-six miles from where he grew up, on a farm where his brother, Frederick, still ran the family business, raising cotton.   Did Will Snow want to be a cotton farmer like that uncle? Perhaps the boy would turn toward religion; be a church leader like his mother, Helen Snow. We might find a clue as to what Will wanted to be by the whimsical playset, 'Mandrake, the Magician' that still held its prominent place in the boy's home-away-from-home, room at his parents' Snow Hotel. Did he perform an astounding trick that transformed him accidently, into a faraway place, where the streets are lined with gold? No one believed for a moment Will wanted to become an angel at the age of sixteen.

In this fiction story, there are two truths to be told:

Mr. and Mrs. William Lafayette Snow came to Grand Saline, Texas and bought a 6 yr. old two-story building on the town square and turned it into 'Hotel Snow and Pharmacy'. He was 31 years of age at the time. Six years later he sold the pharmacy part of the hotel to the Garlands, who were almost as new in town as the Snows were. They named it 'City Pharmacy'. Dr. Garland had his practice upstairs. There remained that empty space at the Snow Hotel where the pharmacy had been. It was turned into a large club room, available to the public. For a price.

The second truth in this book is that Mr. and Mrs. Snow did lose their son when he was sixteen. His heart stopped. So did the world for his parents. The years before and the years after combined, the Hotel Snow was open for business most of forty-two years. Those are truths.

In my fictional story, they choose to go away after the loss of their son, Will, for a while to lick their wounds, mend their hearts. Leave the hotel, with its memories and responsibilities, with caretakers. Close it down to the public. During the following summer months, Mother and Father Snow are gone away, sailing the ocean on Cunard Lines to London, flying Imperial Airways to different foreign countries. Trying desperately to leave their grief behind. Impossibly whiling away the summer of 1938.

CHAPTER 1

   The boy, I will call him 'Will', was only sixteen. His parents, the Snows, could not take their loss and decided to leave the country for an extended trip around the world. At least the wife wanted that. It would be the husband's responsibility to make it happen. He would need to talk to his friends at the Grand Saline First State Bank. They would make all the preparations and arrangements. For a price.

   "Choose several interesting countries, certainly not anywhere near those Hitler has in his eye. There are some who believe Poland won't be enough, that the little man wants all of Europe. Others believe he wants to conquer the world. Some consider him a simple paperhanger and house-painter. We will encounter all views and opinions, traveling. I do not wish to put our lives in danger, so steer clear of Germany, Austria, and certainly Czechoslovakia that he's already wormed us out of. So, choose our itinerary wisely and cautiously, my friend."

William Lafayette Snow was speaking with Preston Powers, the president of First State Bank. Who would bring in a third person, a Mr. Keats, to plan the trip and make reservations, clear pathways, act as travel advisor. He would open doors. Protect the Snows while they were abroad.

The bank would unlock the money.
"You may count on our services."

"Mr. Keats." The president, Preston Powers, called him over with a snap of the wrist. "Mr. Snow would have you begin extensive travel arrangements immediately."

"Yes. Sir.", said Charles Calvin Keats. He knew Mr. Snow and his wife. He knew their circumstances, financially, and personally had known the boy, Will.

"Make the money available. Plenty of it.", demanded Mr. Snow. Easily said, and easily done.

"Let's get you to London first, a luxurious eleven-day voyage on the high seas. Then, fly in luxury with Imperial Airways visiting a wide choice, more than a dozen interesting countries. How does that sound to you?" Mr. Keats was prepared to serve Mr. Snow, and had dozens of exotic travelogues laid out on his desk.

"Do we have to stop at every one?", he asked, knowing his wife would want to.

He gathered the travel folders to take for Mrs. Snow's perusal. She knew where she wanted to go, and he didn't particularly care, so long as it was not in Hitler's path.

The hotel was empty. They never re-opened after the boy died. The town people missed its convenience, a place to stay for visitors from out of town, the dining room for private parties. The club room. They surely missed that club room. The calendar showed reservations made far in advance, now cancelled, crossed out, as calls were made to notify the local clubs, like the Rotary, Lion's Club, the Oddfelllows and Eastern Star for the ladies, that the Hotel Snow, with its amenities, would be closed until further notice. That included its club room, even though, with its outer doors, leading into the alley could have sufficed at least for their intimate Civics Club, or the Boy Scouts to have their meetings. But no. Other plans had been made. That huge room would be living quarters the next few months for relatives who would be occupying that building in the absence of the owners, William and Helen Snow.

An oversized alley separated the hotel and the popular Rayborne Café. They fed the town their meals when wives chose not to cook that day, or an early evening, when men prolonged going home for personal reasons. Perhaps they had been fired that day. The small tables served couples on a date, or one loner. The larger tables served men who gathered at lunch to eat and to talk. They lingered after their meal, for a cigarette or cigar, or to suck on a pipe. They gossiped as much or maybe more than women, each having one eye glued through the front plate glass windows toward the drug store across the street, the post office next to that, or the barber shop, its striped red and white pole in front, turning round slowly, forming an illusion that might hypnotize if one stared long enough. The American flag was proudly on display year around; even when it was not a holiday. The doors of all these businesses constantly opened and closed; anyone coming in or going out would be observed by diners across the street, inside the Rayborne Café.

There would be comments made, often judgements, for or against their friends, neighbors, and strangers. Not pretty girls. They were off limits for comments. They were the daughters or wives of someone who may be sitting at that very table. Expressions might be exchanged. Eyebrows might lift. But words were not spoken about pretty girls who came in and went out all the different doors that opened and closed so many times during an average day.

   That was the view from inside the café. They could see across Frank Street. They could not see the Snow Hotel, beside them, a brick wall in-between. The alley separated those two establishments, the café from the hotel that was, for the time being, closed.

The empty hotel reflected upon the café's profit and loss statement in the files of the First State Bank two doors down from the café. It sat on the corner of Frank Street and Main. Such a lovely street, people walking from the bank to the café, to the Hotel Snow to the service station to the Morton Salt Evaporating Plant.

The alley could have been cleaner. It collected odors. A planted tree in an oversized bucket, concrete poured in the bottom of it, struggled to stand upright and hide the sight. Impossible it was, to stifle the smells. At night, the watchman had his hands full. He carried a blackjack, to run off those hobos who jumped out of the box cars when the Texas and Pacific train pulled its forty cars from Dallas, or the other way coming back from Marshall, the end of the line, running east. That town, Marshall, or rather their sheriff, had run them out of there, and here they came to Grand Saline. Vagrants they were, and plenty of them, broke, hungry, and homeless, even from the depression of 1929; that long. There were no more 'poor houses' to take the indigent. The government, with the act of Social Security in 1935 had closed all of them. So many took to the road or jumped moving trains, going from place to place, looking for somewhere to light. Looking for a home. With the train, its boxcars full of vagrants getting off, asking for a dime, the alley beckoned. It was dark at night. Faster than a light globe could be screwed in, beside the hotel's back door, it was smashed by hoodlums. They went through the garbage from the café. For crumbs. A bite of anything. They could, and did, hide in there. The nightwatchman, given a few extra dollars from merchants, spent more time walking that beat than any other in town. Tapping his hard rubber blackjack against his hand, as a warning, or on the walls of the buildings, running them off should they be huddled in there. He was called 'Early', last name 'Watson'. Who clicked his teeth in dismay, when he raked the broken liquor bottles into a homemade scooper, hoping no child would run through, playing chase perhaps, and get hurt. Children had no business in the alley, but they would come. And they would step on broken glass. Each day the city sent someone out to clean up that alley. They used a mop handle with a nail on the end to stab paper wrappers. They swept the glass into a pile and into buckets, then into the trash cans. Next day, the same routine. But at night more tramps came. It was not unusual for a hotel guest on the second floor to toss an apple core out the window for a bird. Those jumpers from the train hoped they might intercept the toss. They, with their mouths open, like the birds, watered at the thought of a juicy apple core.

   The bums would see the tomato shed first, so close to the train tracks, closer than the cotton gin was. They looked and hoped for forgotten or dropped tomatoes lying by, during that season. The fallen shavings and stems on the ground were picked up and eaten before the sun went down and the moon came up to reveal their appearance in town. They traveled by dark. Safer. Daytimes they still hopped on a boxcar; even sat on the top, hanging on. Not realizing the speed of the moving train, many fell off and were killed. Left for a railway track inspector to discover.

The law would chase them out of town with their clubs. The policemen passed the word that gypsies stayed in the cotton gin building at night. That scared many of them away. Spooked them. They did not consider themselves gypsies, though some lumped all the homeless together in one category.

The Snows arranged for a couple plus household staff, to keep their residence occupied, and regulated, the same as if they, husband and wife, were still sitting at the table three times a day, being served fine food on bone china, and Maxwell House coffee, where the husband might enjoy slurping it from the saucer, just as his own father used to do. His wife, like his mother, would disapprove and then she would have to be reminded, it was he who bought the coffee, and the china, as well as the rich cream that turned it to a chocolate brown instead of black. 'Good to the last drop...and that drop is good too.' The commercial on the Crosley table-top radio guaranteed it to be so. The housekeeper and her husband, the handy man, would run their home place as if their employers were still there. Mr. Snow knew that. That left their hotel's safety to deal with. It could not stand vacant. Not a piece of it would be left when the Snows returned home after a long summer of traveling.

   William Snow had already settled it in his mind, and then he approached his brother in Big Sandy, thirty-six miles east from Grand Saline, where William and Helen lived and ran their Snow Hotel. He asked for help in his situation. He preferred trusted family to care for the hotel in his long absence, rather than paid strangers, or God Help, leaving it locked up, even tightly, with only the nightwatchman to pace up and down and all around. He had promised Early Watson a healthy bonus even exceeding his salary from the city. Still, he wanted family, Snow family, living there, in residence at the hotel.

All in all, the months he planned to be off galivanting around, would cost a great deal of money. He accepted that; would spare no expense. For Helen's sake. He would rather make a deal with his trusted brother to hire his own housekeepers plus at least one member of the immediate family to come and stay to babysit the hotel while they were away. He allowed the worth of such an arrangement, and decided that his brother, so deeply attached to his children, Marilyn, and his namesake whom he called Junior, possessed an ambition for them quite extraordinary, and practically impossible to finance. He would offer Frederick one large sum for their education if they would accept the positions, that of overseeing the Hotel Snow for the summer.

"You know, William", Helen, his wife, reminded him, "the people in Grand Saline would not look upon your brother's household staff with favor, their being Eastern and brown-skinned."

"Good", he exclaimed, with a rare pleasure; there had been none since his son had passed on so unexpectedly. It was his heart. Who knew the boy had an enlarged heart? Certainly not his parents.

"I say good. They'll fear to come around here, doing mischief. The others, my friends in town, will gladly take them in, as gesture to me. Anyway, they owe me the courtesy of respect for my choices. I do enough for this town and the people in it. They better respect my brother's children and those who will be caring for them. Brown or white." He was adamant.

"As you will have it, then.", said his wife. "I just want to leave the worries behind and find tranquility somewhere in this world. Surely one country we plan to visit will offer me solace."

"People in this town have offered you all the understanding they are capable of, Wife. Their patience with us has run out, dealing with their own troubles and sorrows. You know the Jones' lost their son not too long ago. The Smiths' a daughter, and Tom White's whole family was wiped out in that train-car collision at Silver Lake community. They all have their heartaches. Are ours any crueler than theirs?"

"Probably not."

William, with the help of the First State Bank, made all the arrangements. There were many, and with their help, through the president of the bank, their agents, secretaries, managers, and partners, and friends as well, were able to send the Snows on their way, in advance of their replacements. That is, the summer residents. That would be the niece, Miss Marilyn Jane Snow, age twenty-five, never married, her twelve-year-old brother, Junior Snow, named after his father, Frederick Layfayette Snow. They would bring the housemaid, Zasu and her husband, Amm, long faithful couple serving the family. Amm would drive the Model A Ford automobile that would deliver them to Grand Saline, a week after the owners of the Hotel Snow had left the country. The father, and head of that family, Frederick, would settle them in. Go to the bank, follow his brother's instructions, comparing them with his own verbal agreement and consent. Then, if all concerned were settled and planted safely in the Hotel Snow, he would return to the homeplace, to his two younger sons and wife, Margaret, who would probably still be crying twenty-four hours later. She would miss Marilyn and Junior. So would he. But those two of their children, the oldest, would be financially secure at the end of the summer. That was the deal William and Frederick Snow made.

   Zazu and Amm, husband and wife, preferred to stay in Big Sandy, in Upshur County, but their boss, Mr. Frederick Snow, had made a monetary agreement, well in their favor of course, for them to tend to Marilyn and Junior, as all four of them tended the empty Hotel Snow. The couple had never seen it. Had never been to Grand Saline, even though the miles between were only thirty-six.

"I'll see you when I get back.", said Frederick to his wife and two younger sons. He would go to Grand Saline and get Marilyn and Junior, with Amm and Zasu settled in. He would return alone in the Model A Ford to Big Sandy either that night or before daylight.

Also waiting for him at home, in Big Sandy, would be the cotton seeds. He could almost hear them. 'Plant me. Plant me. I want to start my growing process. Be the first load of cotton of the season, brought to the gin. Win the bonus and be on display in the big middle of the town square, with a sign that says, 'The first cotton arriving at the gin, in Van Zandt County, this year 1938'. There would be Frederick Snow's name. First and finest. His cotton was always the finest. He wanted the blue ribbon, the sign that said his name, the pats on his back, the handshakes, the prestige of being exceptional. His own fields were plowed for the cotton seeds to go into the ground. Bad time for this sad business of his nephew, Will, to be taken. He could not and would not refuse his brother's request. He needed help getting his cotton planted. He needed his family intact. They were all helpful during the planting season. Each accepted duty. However, now his brother, William, was asking for his help, and offered cash incentive. With the seed taking 200 days to germinate he hoped and prayed in September his cotton would bring in a good price. With that money plus the cash promised by his brother, William, for the use of his daughter and son's time, as well as his household help (he never called them servants; did not consider them servants), he would be able to put quite a sum away for the education of Junior, his namesake, and the future of Marilyn, whom he expected to stay single forever. She was particular. She did not want a farm boy to marry. She might not want a city boy once she lived among them for a summer. Not that Grand Saline, Texas was a city. It was a nice small town, set upon a salt dome. Most all the boys, upon graduation, worked at the Morton Salt Evaporating Plant in town, or the salt mine five miles south. At least for a while. Some, their entire life. There was a lot of cotton planted and sowed in Van Zandt County as well. Marilyn would have both cotton farmers and salt miners to choose from, realized her father. Maybe she would marry after all.

CHAPTER 2.

Amm is driving the car. He is a slender, slight man, and quite dark. He is of East Indian descent. He has excellent presence in any situation, prideful, self-assured. He is a man of few words. His ears are sharp of hearing, pointed in design. He has dark hair rarely seen from under a well-fitted gangster-style fedora with a band of grosgrain ribbon, black and white stripe. Now his head grazed the roof of the Model A Ford automobile. He was that tall.

Admittedly mysterious, he could be standing in a room, and one would be astonished at his silent presence, wondering how he got there, and how long he'd been there. How much had he heard?

'Everything', would be the answer. Today he is behind the wheel of the automobile, at its owner's request. Beside him, the shift separating them, sits Frederick Snow, who is dressed well, wearing his best suit and tie, shoes polished to a high shine. He will don his own modest hat when he leaves the car. He intends to make a good impression on those who requested he come directly to the bank. He wonders if he will be greeted by the president himself. Well, he would think so. His brother, William Lafayette Snow practically owned that bank. He had heard his brother claim he did.

William certainly did not own the First State Bank. However, he was a heavy investor. He carried a lot of weight.

Frederick intended to go there, collect the keys to the Hotel Snow, and a package of papers and instructions. He would be given a blank check book for expenses and lists of stores he could patronize and simply say, 'Charge it.' Not him, of course, but his daughter, Marilyn. She would be the one running things, writing checks, saying, 'Charge it.' for groceries and other needs.

   She would go into the bank with him, to exchange introductions, and do what business needed to be done. He wanted to get it over with, then go take a look at his brother's hotel (he had not been there in a long time). He hoped it would be in good repair; had not brought any tools. Amm would be expected to keep things up. He was good at fixing things. In fact, sometimes it looked as if he simply waved a magic wand, and it was done.

In the back seat are Marilyn and Zazu, with Junior. Who is wearing his 'hero suit', loose-fitting white shirt and pants, yellow and red cummerbund tied around his waist, and white turban wrapped around his head. There was no time for his father to make him change to suitable clothes before the boy was seated in the backseat between Marilyn and Zazu. Some things are not so important. Scolding Junior and sending him back inside to change clothes, with his mother beginning the crying goodbyes all over again was not worth it. He let it go.

Zasu and Amm thoroughly approved the boy's choice of comic hero, as well as his mode of dress, his costume of 'Punjab' from 'Little Orphan Annie', comic strip and radio fame. They would approve, being Pakistani Indian themselves.

Amm is driving. His small round dark eyes miss nothing. His pointy ears hear whispers as easily as shouts. To others, he is considered a strange one. To the Snow family, he is indispensable. Quiet and reserved, he aims to please. He fits in like a hand does a glove, comfortable, warm, and safe. Zazu and Amm have been with the Snows, in Big Sandy, Texas, forever. To Marilyn and Junior, they are an integral part of the family. They will feel completely safe in the capable hands of that couple.

    During the drive to Grand Saline, Frederick Snow is not worrying about that. He appears irritated because the cotton seeds are waiting, to be planted in his fields. He had seen to the preparation. He had his people at the ready. He could not be gone past tomorrow. He wished Amm would drive faster.

    Zazu is calm. She, like Amm, come from good ancestry. They have always lived in America in East Texas. Their parents had been friends, had come together, as immigrants from Pakistan. Became citizens of the United States. She and Amm were bound together since childhood, had married, had taken their place in the household of Frederick and Margaret Snow. They retain their mysterious Indian heritage as best and conveniently as possible. It was not always so. They have run into problems of acceptance, yes, even in their hometown of Big Sandy. They are used to handling suspicion and skepticism. They have risen above most of it.

Was their Indian influence the source of Junior Snow originating his 'hero image'? That of 'Punjab'? He wore that type of clothes. Long soft pants, shirt of the same whiteness, the turban of the same fabric wrapped around his head. Amm does not wear the headdress. Punjab loves wearing one. He is waiting for the perfect decoration to pin on the front of his turban. It must have both beauty and meaning. Something brilliant that sparkles when the sun hits it. When he finds the right 'jewel' he will pin it on. He wears shoes today. He usually runs around barefoot. His father had not made him go change clothes. Maybe because he was at least wearing shoes.

No. it was not the influence of Amm, nor Zazu that Junior chose this attire. He was pretending to be 'Punjab', from the comic figures of Harold Gray's 'Little Orphan Annie', in books, magazines and on radio. His parents thought it was alright that he chose to be that hero. He could have chosen to be a villain. At least, Punjab was a good influence on a boy of twelve.

Junior, or rather Punjab, sits beside Zazu, her dark black hair pinned back in a tight plait, her dark eyes peering out the window behind a silk scarf. She wears modest clothing, practical, perhaps longer skirts, higher blouses than moderns, with shawls of color around her shoulders.

   The automobile, with her husband at the steering wheel is driving them to Grand Saline, Texas, where she has never been. She observes all she can see. That's what she habitually does, observe, before reacting. Her parents had taught her to do that. They had been proven right most of the time. Highway 80 splits Big Sandy Lake, right in the middle. They are past that. They are less than thirty miles to Grand Saline.

CHAPTER 3

   There were many people who stared at them in an automobile, with suitcases, trunks and packages tied tightly to its sides, rear and top, every item wrapped solidly, immovable as the wheels rolled down the highway. Somehow, they had managed to tie Junior's bicycle on the back. The boy had to have a way to get around during the summer. A boy could not stay cooped up in a hotel room. Not Junior anyway. The automobile wheels rolled west. Marilyn read every sign. And marveled. Punjab asked if he could ride into town on the fender and wave at the people on the streets.

"You mean like a parade, Son? You look like a parade in progress, dolled up in that suit." Frederick tried to sound stern. It was hard. Junior was a good boy. His boy. His son. His brother had lost his son, Will. He still had his, here, asking to ride on the fender in a parade of one automobile. What harm could that do? So, he agreed.

"But only through that one block, Son."

He did object to the way Junior was dressed. He intended to get him inside the hotel before everyone in town began making fun of him. Junior would be unaware of any slight. Much too happy a boy to notice one.

   Amm turned left at Highway 80 at the traffic light and 110. They were in Grand Saline. Cars were parked in front of the stores and in the middle of the street. There was a picture show and the sign read, 'The Grand Theatre' Practically new it was only nine months old. Still long enough to have a name change. It was, at first, 'The Palace Theatre'.

   "Stay on this main street. Go on past the bank. I want to take a look at their cotton gin on the other side of the railroad tracks."

   At the wheel, Amm followed instructions. He saw the train depot on the left He saw no train coming from east nor west, so he drove over the tracks. The cotton gin was closed. They saw the tomato shed nearby. It had a little activity; men working; making repairs from the previous season, getting it ready for Spring to settle in, tomatoes to appear in abundance.

"Turn back around, Amm. If you keep going, you'll end up at the salt mine, about five miles farther. You all will have plenty of time to see that. I want my boy to go down into that mine. He'll be amazed. But right now, we have to get to the bank. Get that over with."

Frederick's mind stayed on what he had just seen, the cotton gin. It was a fine one. There were plenty of cotton gins. A farmer would have to travel only three to five miles to get to one, with his load. This one was thirty-six miles from home, Big Sandy, but would be convenient anyway, if he could deliver his cotton at the same time that he came back to retrieve his brood, the kids and Amm and Zazu, his household help. Then, when he went back home, he would have one pocket full of pay for the cotton, after ginning, and the other pocket full of cold cash from his brother for his children and his household help for the three months overseeing the Snow Hotel.

  "Put the boy on the fender." He had promised. Punjab could see everything, and over the rooftops of the stores he saw the Hotel Snow sign on a two-story building. It was impressive enough but there was a bigger sign that advertised Morton Salt next door. Amm drove slowly. They returned the stares of the people on the streets. In awe. Everyone was looking at their loaded down automobile. On top were suitcases. On the back was a trunk. And a bicycle. Packages were stacked up against the windows, inside, and faces appeared from behind them. Punjab was riding on the fender when the car came to a full stop in front of the First State Bank. His father had allowed him that. This would be the last time he would see his son, until after cotton was harvested. The boy would be denied the honor of riding into town to declare the harvested cotton the first in the county to be brought to the gin. He would have allowed his son to sit on top of the sacks of cotton. So, Frederick let Junior ride, today, on the fender of the Model A, instead. All the people in town were staring at the overgrown boy dressed in a 'Little Orphan Annie' costume; one of Punjab, her bodyguard. They probably caught a glimpse of the dark lady behind her scarf, taking up the space that Punjab had vacated. He was sitting now on the fender of the automobile as it glided softly into the parking space in front of the bank and quietly, the motor shut off. The silence was deadly. They were left with feelings of not being welcome in Grand Saline, Texas.

Frederick Snow sizzled. How dare they peer into his car... meddle in his family business? The town is small. There is a square. The bank sits on the corner. It is two-story. Well built.

Frederick offered his arm to his daughter. Amm and Zasu would stay where they were. They would wait.

"Get down. Get in the car.", Frederick told his son. Reluctantly, Junior jumped off the fender and Zazu opened the door, hurrying him in, settling him in. As his father had seen, a lone photographer from the local newspaper was hurrying toward them, but he would be denied a photograph of his son dressed up as Punjab.

Marilyn went into the bank with her father, not prominent nor rich as his brother in Grand Saline, but not poor either. He drove an automobile as fine as he. He had land, valuable land with rich soil, abundant cotton crops every year, a nice home, practically paid for, and current taxes paid. The cotton farmer wanted the banker to recognize his status and know the value of cotton and land. He was dressed well. He spoke well. He came to collect keys, he told Mr. Keats who led him into the office of the president of the bank. There would be an exchange of signatures, for blank checks, important authoritative papers, some petty cash money. And keys to the hotel would be handed over.

   Mr. Keats, the young man, stood beside the older one, Preston Powers, the president, who held out his hand in welcome. Keats did not miss the beauty of the daughter, Marilyn Snow. His underarms began to perspire. He kept them down. She was marvelous. She could not help but notice and lowered her eyes. It was as if she were in a movie, where a gentleman kisses the hand of a lady. She wanted to offer hers. But no. That was only for the movies. Mr. Powers was mouthing words. She was glad her daddy was taking care of business because she could not hear nor speak. She was breathless. Was this how it felt to fall in love at first sight?

Finally, after a time, Mr. Keats walked out of the bank with Marilyn. A camera snapped their picture. The reporter from the Grand Saline Sun offered his card, taken from the band of his hat. It read, 'Warren Wright, reporter'.

"Could I have another?", he asked Marilyn.

"Another picture? Horrors no." She primped.

Out came Frederick with keys. Punjab was introduced to Mr. Keats, as his son. He would be running errands, representing the Snow family. Frederick took pains to introduce Amm. Who did not know he was on the authorized list of the bank to also represent the Snows. Frederick made that clear. He would make many trips to the bank and should be welcomed as if he were the head of the household. His wife, Zasu was introduced as well. It was necessary to accept each one of their presence in town. Frederick knew his brother, the owner of the hotel, William Lafayette Snow, had made those demands in person and on paper. The bank was the first establishment to lay down a welcome mat for those Snows who came to their town, directly from Big Sandy, Texas. And to treat the Indian people who came with them respectfully.

Zazu slanted her eyes, knowing, at least feeling, the attraction between the banker, Mr. Keats, and Marilyn. She was and had always been protective of her. It would be necessary for the next three months for her to continue to be vigilant.

"Are you still here?", Frederick asked the newspaper reporter. He was writing down every bit of information exchanged. It would appear in the next edition of the Grand Saline Sun. Readers were curious and would expect answers. Sales would hit the roof. And the byline would be his. It would read, 'by Warren Wright'. Who stood there, pen in hand.

"Sir, If I could just ask you…"

"No."

But Marilyn thought her dad was unduly harsh. She cushioned his remark with an apologetic smile. He colored, not surprisingly from the noonday sun that skipped across her blonde tresses, turning a few selected hairs a golden color. Her eyes appeared to change from green to match the gold. Marilyn had won the hearts of two eligible young men in Grand Saline, Texas, and she had been there less than an hour.

The hotel was a few doors down from the bank, but Frederick wanted to see a bit of the town first. Amm drove north, crossed

Highway 80. The Christian Church was on the right. The Baptist Church on the left.

Frederick told them he expected them to be in church every Sunday morning; the Baptist Church, though his sister-in-law had suggested they go to the Christian Church. It would become the beginning of the Church of Christ, in Grand Saline later. Helen Snow would be one of its most prominent members.

"Further up the street is the school. You won't be going there. Turn around here. Let's go back through town." On their right, was the 'Grand' theater. He told them they could go to the movies sometimes.

"It looks presentable", he said, "Only not on Sundays. That is a day of reflection, of rest, of prayer." Amm drove past the movie house and turned right on Frank Street at the intersection. The bank was on their left. He could see the 'Hotel Snow' sign, and the alley where he would pull in, to unload their belongings. Out of sight of the public's eye.

"Leave everything. We will walk in the front door, civilized, make sure these are the right keys. We won't stand there, airing our packages of nightclothes while I fiddle with a key that might not work."

The front door was the hotel lobby, serviceable and comfortable to check in guests. The double doors led into a dining room that could be seen from outside, with almost all windowpanes from floor to ceiling. There were long tables with crisp cloths of white, and many chairs.

Frederick could not resist reminding his daughter that the chairs and matching Italian credenza were in his brother's will; they would go to her, Marilyn, who had admired them once a long time ago, when she came to Grand Saline, for a visit, to play with their son, her cousin, Will. Frederick lowered his voice, as if ghosts in the hotel were listening and would tattle to its owners about wills and bequeaths.

He said to her, "You may be in receipt of this furniture sooner than you think, Child. I don't believe they will ever feel comfortable on these premises again, with their son, gone. They may sell the hotel."

The credenza held no decoration. A ceiling fan was gently circling. It had started when the light switch was turned on. Frederick turned off the light switch, and the fan quit. He closed the double doors. Beyond the staircase that led to the hotel rooms upstairs, was a sink and toilet, for dining guests. The spacious kitchen was fully stocked in anticipation of the family's arrival. A door led to the clubroom. They all walked through. It was huge; would be their living area. The clubroom had been turned into a family room for their benefit. The furniture still had plastic covering the new sofas and chairs.

"You will live in this room. You will sleep in the bedrooms upstairs. You will eat in the kitchen. You will not disturb the dining room. People outside will be looking in through all those windows. They would see you as a moving picture show. You will act discreetly, knowing that you represent the Snow family. Both his and mine. Now, we go upstairs to choose bedrooms." Frederick had spoken.

Marilyn wanted the smaller one, the sunniest. It had a balcony. Perfect for her. The bed and chest were good wood pieces. Money had been spent on thick rugs. Amm and Zazu chose the bedroom adjacent to Marilyn's because of the extended balcony.

Will's room, still as it was when he passed on, was off limits. It stayed the way he left it. Will spent many nights at the hotel, by choice sometimes, by necessity other times. He had accumulated quite a lot of personal belongings, with hobbies and games and books. His mother would not let anyone touch them and they lay as he left them. The door was locked.

"May I live in here?", Junior wanted the room across from Will's. His dad looked it over, and asked him did he really want to be so far from the others? He did.

"I 'spect you'll change your mind after a night or two. This place has its share of rattles and echoes." He turned to all of them and announced his immediate plans.

"I will sleep in the room with Junior. Not to mess up the other bedrooms for such a small part of the night. I'll be leaving in the wee hours to return home. Amm, come go with me. We will go to my brother's home and take a look at the vehicle you are to have access to, for the benefit of the family.

Only during the day will it be driven and only for good purpose. Every night the car will be returned to its garage. You will walk back the two blocks to the hotel. I say this because it might not be safe parked on the street at night. Certainly not kept in that filthy alley. I don't like mine parked there even for the short time I'll be here. Come, everyone, we will unpack the car."

"Can't we eat first?" begged Junior.

"Everyone will work. Then everyone will eat.", said the father.

CHAPTER 4

They stood on the balcony; all of them. The scene was the Morton Salt Evaporating Plant. It was active with the nightshift. One would expect to hear loud noise, but not this day. Not this evening. The 300 ft. tall smokestack was bellowing white smoke, its purpose was to keep pollution from the population, the chimney pipes releasing combustion air gases, carbon dioxide and water vapor.

  Ironically, the smokestack was a beacon for airplanes. It reassured the pilots were headed the right direction. One such plane chose that moment to fly over, and the silence of the night was interrupted with the harsh sound of its engines. Words were stifled until it flew over. The balcony was situated where part of the town's stores and establishments were visible, if it were daytime, and during summer months when it was still light outside until after eight. Now, at this hour, lights were being shut off, one by one, and little by little it darkened. There was no light on the balcony where the family gathered for one last time before Frederick would leave them. He asked his children if all they saw displayed, along with the endless sky, didn't make them feel small and insignificant.

"In God's Eyes, we are each of us here to serve his purpose. We have been called to this place, this town, this time to help one fellow man, who happens to be my brother...your uncle, in his heartbreak, the loss of his son. We are bound to do our best. I expect no less from you, my children. We will hold hands and pray. For safety, for success, for the blessings and mercies from the Lord." He explained they could come out on the other end, at the close of summer, well endowed. They must stick together. Get through the next 3 months. Finally, he said, "Your mother and your brothers and I will miss you."

They looked down, suddenly, and saw the nightwatchman's flashlight pointed in their direction.

The father said, "Make friends with him. Your life may depend on it."

Early Watson, the nightwatchman, saw them gathered on the balcony. He did not wave. He stepped on a stray cat who screamed. He told the cat he was sorry.

Junior slept soundly. His dad slept beside him until the hour to leave for home...Big Sandy. He rose, stood there solemnly a moment. He watched him sleep, listened to his breathing. It was even. The boy was content. He covered him, drawing the cool sheet up to his chin. He kissed him on his forehead and left.

Early Watson, the nightwatchman had gone home. The sun had been up for a good while, but everyone was still asleep except for Junior Snow. He wanted to check out the stores on the square. He dressed, as usual, as Punjab. The one store that he wanted to go into was the 'City Pharmacy' drug store, across the street from the hotel. He expected it would have magazines and comic books. Where there were comic books, there would the latest edition of 'Little Orphan Annie'. And she would have need of Punjab to protect her. He was her bodyguard. She had a small dragon's tail whistle. Punjab gave to her. She should blow it anytime she needed him. When she needed him no more, she would say, simply, 'I wish to be alone.' And Punjab would disappear. Junior Snow had such a whistle. He had written off to the Ovaltine company and sent a box top and a dime for the premium. The dragon looked peaceful. Playful. He wondered if, by magic, he could give it a fiercer image. He tried out a few magic words, but they did not work. He would try many others.

   This fine morning, he sat on the floor of the drug store, reading the comic book he hoped they would have, 'Little Orphan Annie'. A girl, a bit younger than he, sat down beside him. He looked up at her, with her orange hair and thought she looked like Little Orphan Annie...a little.

"What's left, at the end of the month, those that don't sell, I get to keep free. My cousin works here. She's a soda jerk at the fountain. At the end of the month, she tears off the covers of magazines nobody buys. She sends them back to the company for a refund. The store lets her take the rest of the magazine, or comic books, without the covers, home with her. She saves the comics for me."

Junior Snow did not respond.

"People in this town are not really into Little Orphan Annie, I don't think, because there's always some of those left. I have a lot. I get the comic books", the little girl explained. "Rachel keeps the movie magazines. That's my cousin."

"Wow. How lucky you are, I mean to get them free. I like Orphan Annie because of Punjab. He's her bodyguard and protects her. He's really neat. But I like other comics.

A boy about Junior's age and who resembled the little girl joined them. He sat on the floor alongside.

"Say, why are you dressed up like the character in Little Orphan Annie, the one called Punjab?"

"Who said I was dressed like him? Maybe he's dressed like me." He said it with humor, open to meeting someone his own age. The little girl might be okay, owning comic books and all, but it was a boy pal he needed, to run around town with. To ride bicycles with.

'My name is Harry Dunne. She's my little sister, Deane Dunne. Our cousin is a soda jerk here. She gives us ice cream cones sometimes when the boss is not looking. Like he's not here now or else he wouldn't let us sit on his floor and read the comic books free."

"I'm going to buy one. I have money.", said Junior. "By the way, both of you...I would prefer you call me Punjab. I kinda don't like what folks who know me, call me, which is Junior. My dad is Frederick Snow."

He was standing now, with a comic book in one hand, his other poked in his pocket, bringing forth coins his dad had given him for pocket money.

Harry Dunne asked him if he was with the hotel people and was told yes.

CHAPTER 5

Marilyn, with her companions, Amm and Zasu, would venture out for the first time, not counting the previous stop at the First

State Bank on arrival day. They would go next door to the Rayborne Café, knowing they would be accepted there. Her uncle had made sure. He had arranged to be sent a total bill for all charges while they occupied the hotel. The café would benefit considerably.

Marilyn went into the dining room, to get a full view out the plate glass windows, of the townspeople walking past the hotel, or across the street. Who traded curiosities, peering in at her. She wore a pale-yellow morning dress with a soft peplum at the waist and a spring cloche. Was lovely even without makeup. She wanted a moment all to herself, before going outside. The three of them would have a good hearty breakfast.

Now she leaned on one of the dining room chairs. They were to be hers. Now what on earth would she do with fourteen dining room chairs and one credenza, that she faintly recalled admiring once upon a time long ago when she had been invited to spend a summer with Uncle William and Aunt Helen, and her cousin Will? Why were there fourteen chairs? Why not sixteen? That would even out to six to each of three six- foot tables set up in the room. Had time killed off those two? Had they come to a bad ending? Had they been used as weapons? She imagined a fight like in a western movie where cowboys broke chairs over heads. Not in here. This dining room was a place of elegance, fine food., good manners.

And how about the tables? Who got them? In the will, who got the tables? She would get the credenza. The huge credenza that held silverware that clinked against each other as they were taken from the drawer, along with the crisp linen napkins, to place on the tables and in the laps of those who came there to dine. The clientele, equally hotel guests and townspeople, with those passing through, leaving highway 80 at the traffic signal to enter the town square, looking for a place to get a bite. The charming Snow Hotel beckoned, with promises of lovely food served on white linen tablecloths and oversized, napkins, real honest to goodness silver spoons, forks and knives, and an elegant chair to sit on, to enjoy the pleasurable atmosphere.

   Once hers, she could sell the chairs to an antique shop. She wanted that credenza. With all her heart, she believed, had always believed, that it was magical. How else could those silver spoons forks and knives (she remembered were embossed with grapes by design on the handles), ring and ting-a-ling against each other with such musical sounds as they were lifted out of the drawer for service? She remembered that today.

She heard Will tell the story of the gold coin. Grandpa's coin that went missing. Could not be found. He did not say he thought it might be in the credenza, but had that thought injected into her mind at the time she was told the story.

Long ago, Will's grandfather, (and her own), took his cotton all the way from Big Sandy to Louisiana to be ginned, hoping to get more pay for such fine cotton. They gave him a one- hundred- dollar gold piece for it. To his grave he never spent that gold coin. Years later the old man whispered in the ear of William where the coin was. And died a short time after. Her own dad never asked what happened to the coin. He knew his brother would relish his asking, but pride held him back. He was jealous.

William got the coin, the formal education with all its privileges. He became a pharmacist. And later a hotelier. He wore fine clothes, was invited to be a member of the town's prestigious men's clubs. Had dinner often with the president of the bank, in his home.

But that was a long time ago. Little of childish jealousies remained between Frederick and his brother, William Snow.

When Marilyn was with Will and heard the story, she thought the coin might be in that credenza and so did he. But that furniture was heavy and lay flat on the floor. They took everything out of its drawers, silverware, linen, doilies. It was still immoveable. They put everything back where it belonged, and the coin was not mentioned again.

Chapter 6

Marilyn Snow caused quite the stir when word circulated she had arrived in Grand Saline. One would think she had come for a premiere at the picture show, the 'Grand

Theater'. Or perhaps to film a movie. Who was she?

"Did you hear? That Snow woman has moved into the hotel."

"What Snow woman?"

"The one who really owns the Snow Hotel."

I thought Helen and William Snow owned the Snow Hotel."

"She is a Snow. They say she is 'blood kin'.

"Far as I know the Snows had only that one child, Will, who died recently."

"She came here one time, to play with the boy. I think she is a niece from Big Sandy."

"They say she's delicate, that the sun has never touched her skin, 'white as snow'. My husband called her 'Lady Snow.' He saw her come out of the bank, escorted out by Preston Powers himself."

"The president of the bank. She's here to lay claim on that hotel, the land it sits on, right smack-dab in our town square."

"I heard she's going to open it back up. The ladies in town say she's going to rent it out to single ladies only. Right here in front of our very own eyes. Do you think so?"

"As much true as those claims she's going to run a gambling hall in it.", retorted one man who was listening to the ladies go on about Marilyn Snow. The women, in unison, 'harrumphed' and continued wagging their tongues.

Inside the café the talk was all about the new occupants of the hotel. It was understood that they would be eating all their meals there, free of charge, paid in advance by William Snow, and be free to run up charge accounts all over town for whatever they wanted. Someone remarked that poor Ms. Bertha Carpenter would be running up and down the stairs of the hotel, delivering her pies and cakes and they would probably not be obliged to tip her a nickel. Who was slicing generous pieces of her latest creation, caramel cake, the topping still hot and oozing down the sides. She made no comment. It would not be proper for her to do so. She was the cook and baker of the café. Tattle tales in the café told all they heard. That the drug store would remain open day and night for their convenience and whims, and the doctor and dentist at their disposal. The grocery store had an unlimited charge account set up for them.

"That Mr. Keats, at the First State Bank will be standing on the corner issuing out dollar bills to that kid for him to spend at the five and dime, buying Balsam airplane kits and wind-up rubber wheeled tractors."

Someone tittered, "Or rubber dollies."

Ms. Bertha had to speak up on that one. That stepped over the line, inferring the boy was a sissie.

"I know for a fact that the nephew of Mr. Snow, is a fine boy. I, for one, will be kind to all of them for taking care of the hotel, after what they have gone through, losing their boy." That shut them up for the time being.

Some of the gossip was true. During this period, the young lady, Marilyn, would be overseeing expenses and checks. Amm had been authorized to act as a transport between the girl and the bank, but not for great sums of cash. There would be no need of that. The Snows had complete trust in

Amm and Zasu. The town would take its time warming up to that couple. For now, most would reserve their opinion.

  The banker, Mr. Keats, was thrilled to be the center of attention when he went into the café to get his first cup of coffee for the day. He had a lot to tell and was willing to share all of it without disclosing bank business. By nature, he was outgoing, and talkative. Today was no exception. In the middle of a story, the front door to the café opened and there were three coming in who would object to his telling anything about them. They were Marilyn, with Amm and his wife and companion, Zasu. Mr. Keats looked rather sheepish. He should be more loyal to that beautiful sensitive girl. He loved her wearing the yellow dress.

  They had a fine breakfast. Homemade biscuit, local butter, and honey. Sliced tomatoes. Fried bacon for Marilyn. None of that for the Indians. They did drink the sweet milk offered, with rich cream in their coffees. They were Americanized in most ways but refused pork. The cook, Mrs. Bertha Carpenter, saw to them personally and told them they had a running account that would be taken care of by the hotel owners. They should come often, eat well and to call on the phone for deliveries should they not feel up to coming into the café. When they stood up to leave, Ms. Bertha, brought forth her new specialty, a strawberry pie with whipped cream piled high on top. She insisted they take it home, to the hotel, with her compliments, free of charge. Bertha told anyone who came in and who cared to listen that those three had acted dignified and courteous in the café. That couldn't be said about a lot of the townspeople who took up desirable tables smoking their stinky cigars and making fun of those walking down the sidewalks outside. There was one child who wore roller skates inside the café. She had no consideration. No manners at all.

"Know what that kid did? She ate her ice cream cone with her skate key."

Mr. Keats had left, looking guilty after talking about them. He had tipped his hat and backed out of the café, forgetting his take-out coffee.

Zasu would accompany Marilyn, when she left the hotel, at least for a few days. She was safe. Everyone in town knew those people from the Snow Hotel were protected by the prominent president of the Chamber of Commerce, and the proprietor of the Snow Hotel. He owned an interest in the bank. The people in Grand Saline knew better than to cross any of his family. That included Amm and Zasu, those 'strange' people of India.

During the first week, there was not one store Punjab did not go into, though he bought nothing. Not one balsam airplane, wind-up rubber wheeled tractor, or rubber dolly. He answered to 'Punjab' and answered to 'Junior' not at all. He had friends, the two Dunnes. Mostly the boy. The girl, Deane, did not have a bicycle and her sidewalk roller skates, the kind that used a 'key' did not travel fast enough to keep up with the overactive boys. Not that she didn't try. Then, they would leave the sidewalk and go where her skates were not allowed to take her.

So far Punjab had not been invited to the Dunne home. He would be, finally, to come see Deane's dog she wanted to pass off as 'Annie's dog, Sandy', from the comic strip. The boys would have to accept her as their beloved Annie if they expected to have her dog as 'Sandy'. She intended to be a part of it all, but the boys rejected both of them.

Her mother, Mrs. Dunne, was kind enough. Her children liked Junior Snow. That family was highly regarded. She gave a party for Deane, and invited several children, including Junior Snow. He came, dressed in his hero suit, all in white including turban and Deane was more determined than ever to be his 'Annie' from the comic strip.

"Why can't I be Annie, with you and my brother?", Deane Dunne asked. "I could provide the Sandy dog."

"Why your dog is not even yellow. He's not even big. He's spotted. Black and white spotted, and he doesn't take directions well. He jumps up and scratches my ankles and tries to tear my pants.", Junior, as Punjab, argued.

Amm drove Junior where he wanted to go. He had his bicycle of course and there was nowhere in Grand Saline that was too far to go on a bicycle. The reason Amm drove him around was so Junior, as Punjab, could pretend to be chauffeured by 'Daddy

Warbucks' personal bodyguard, 'The Asp', as in Little Orphan Annie. Punjab would sit in the backseat and pretend. He dressed the part.

Amm looked his part all the time, wearing his gangster-style fedora, a lengthwise crease in the crown, two slight front pinches, and a grosgrain ribbon around the band. He was 'authentic'.

Amm had a good time being 'The Asp'. He had never read a comic book that told him how 'The Asp' would act, but had a pretty good idea, protecting, not 'Daddy Warbucks', but Punjab. That was his job, in reality.

Together they explored the town. They drove up and down streets, looked at homes and parks. At the church, Amm saw a lot of boys and girls who were Junior's age.

"Looks like they're having 'vacation bible school'. Do you want to sign up for that? It might be fun."

"I don't think I want to spend my vacation going to school.", he said.

"Very well.", said Amm.

They viewed the schools and sports fields. They sat on a wooden bench and watched the birds. Punjab climbed the slide, slid down, adjusted his turban, chinned on the bars, adjusted his turban again, while hanging from his toes. Sometimes the turban was a drawback. He handed his dragon whistle to Amm and told him to blow it when it was time to go. He climbed a tree and sat there a long while. Until Amm blew the whistle and Punjab appeared quickly.

"This town is pretty tame, isn't it?"

"It is whatever you make of it, P.J."

That was the first time anyone called him P.J. He liked it. He would be P.J. when he was not being 'Punjab.' He decided at that moment.

They drove into the country, saw the farmhouses, their barns, plowed fields, some already had planted their cotton; some not yet, but had their rich dirt ready and waiting. Quilts on the line flared in the gentle wind, and white crisp sheets flapped, making a cracking sound he was familiar with, that of his mother hanging her freshly washed sheets. P.J. would not admit to missing his mother. He was expected to rise to the occasion. Help babysit his uncle's hotel for the summer.

"They hang their underwear and petticoats next to overalls and work shirts.

Kinda uneven looking. Mama would not do that.", said P.J.

There were plenty of outhouses to be seen beside the houses. Not all homes had indoor plumbing at that time in 1938. They had water wells with pumps. They used butane gas for heating.

Buttercups were plentiful in the fields and Indian blankets. Bluebonnets covered the ground on each side of the roads. Outside the city limits there were lean-to stands, run by farmers to sell their fruits and vegetables. Tomatoes were plump and red in baskets. They would take some to Marilyn and Zasu.

Coming home, Amm drove past the Morton Salt Mine and asked P.J. if he wanted to go down in the ground, inside the dome of salt. He would go with him.

"Yes. I would like that, but not today.

"Does it sound dangerous to you?", he asked his little charge.

"Are you kidding? Punjab will go down there. Dangerous to Punjab? Punjab not afraid of anything." He continued acting brave.

"I will go down there. I will drive out any evil that lurks in the shadows of the halls. I will chase them through the tunnels, and caverns, pound them with great chunks of salt. I will drive the tractors over them and pin them to the walls where they will melt into oblivion, I am the great Punjab." He beat his chest. Amm saw that P.J. had been versed on the wonders the salt mine held; caverns, tunnels, walls of solid salt.

Machines taken down the elevator in pieces were put back together again, and trucks the same, that drove through the halls of solid salt. He had never gone down in the mine, but believed it was much like the halite salt mines in his birth country, Pakistan. There the salt was of a pinkish to beet red color. He had read books and seen pictures but had not seen them. He was brought to America when a baby. Here, white salt was in every shaker on every table. The blue and white salt box had a little girl on the front, their logo, sprinkling salt as she walked along, carrying an umbrella, with the words written, 'When it rains, it pours.'

He drove on and noticed tents going up, two miles from town, between the salt mine and the train depot. There was a carnival setting up. He didn't like that. Con artists invaded every carnival. The hawkers cheated the children out of their pennies they threw in jars, for a prize. Or shot a duck off the ledge, threw a ball or a beanbag. They displayed large stuffed animals to be won yet rewarded the winners with small junk toys that came apart before they left the booth. They ruined the fun for the children. The parents could not afford kids' rides and games during this time, in 1938, barely out of a long depression, shortly into a possible military conflict with Germany. He took the boy back to the hotel. He would return alone to pay a visit with the carnival people.

The following morning, they were gone, as they came, without fanfare. Amm had offered them a little friendly persuasion.

CHAPTER 7

"Can Harry spend the night?", P.J. wanted to know. The name, or rather initials, had stuck.

"I don't see why not.", Marilyn said. Plans were made for the following night.

He brought his genuine mystifying oracle talking board with planchette. Some called it an Ouija board. It was proposed that one could use it to contact the dead. No one knew he had it in his night case. Marilyn would have objected. She didn't believe that evil hid inside a board game but did not take chances. She was not aware one such board was brought into the hotel room of P.J.s to play with, when darkness came.

That day, the mail man brought several letters from Big Sandy, with news from home, and then another brought packages from overseas. They were addressed to the hotel, in care of Marilyn Snow, Obviously the sender, Mrs. Helen Snow, preferred them to be stored at the hotel rather than her home. Marilyn had been told to put them into one of the hotel rooms. She chose to put them in Will's. It was always locked. She took a key from the desk in the office, that would unlock his room. She had the packages in hand.

P.J. saw her opening his door, from his own room across the hall. He asked if he could look inside. Marilyn saw no harm in that. She opened the door wide so that P.J. could get a good overall look. He only said one word under his breath. It was, "Wow." Neat it was, bedspread on the bed, a green shaded reading lamp on a side table. Eyeglasses as he had left them when he went to sleep that night. There was a pigskin football on the dresser. A photo of Will, holding one like it stood in a silver frame. He was a sports' fella, P.J. realized. No one had told him that. In fact, no one had told him anything about his cousin, except that he was sixteen and died. Of course, P.J. had never asked for details.

It was a boy's room, there for Will's pleasure while he stayed at the hotel when his dad and mom were working there. There were books and puzzles, and the largest glass jar of marbles P.J. had ever seen. Quite the collection. The walls held personal framed photographs One was of Will, suit and tie, a girl beside him wearing a corsage of flowers. They both had crowns. He couldn't read the banner. They must have been given an honor, that of King and Queen of something.

   Suddenly P.J. saw it. The most magnificent image. The cover of a boxed game. It was on a shelf with others, Flinch, Chinese checkers, Parcheesi. It was a 'Mandrake, the Magician Magic Set.' He lost his voice. It couldn't be. Will Snow was into the comic book character, 'Mandrake, the Magician.' After a few moments, his sister closed the door to Will's room. She locked it, the postal packages in a neat stack on the floor where she had decided to store them, for now.

CHAPTER 8

   Mandrake, the Magician made its appearance the same year that Little

Orphan Annie did, in 1924. It was not an adventure series particularly, but that of a magician of mystery.

   He wore a top hat, a black cape with a bright red lining. He carried a cane that gave him magical powers, a stage magician who possessed real magic no one suspected he had. A master of illusion he could send out vibes and make people see things that weren't there. He used it on villains like 'the Cobra.', an Ice Robot. He was P.J.'s second favorite comic book hero, and practiced magic card tricks, and would try to make magic happen, simply by concentration and willing it to happen. That had been the advice from Zasu. She could cause objects to move. Little ones. P.J. suspected it was not magic but trickery. If he could not master magic, he would learn trickery he finally decided after Zasu fooled him once too often.

"Rise", she said to one of her life size marionette dolls she kept. She put on plays for the family sometimes.

"Rise, I command you." Again, she tapped her baton against the form that lay flat on the floor. She raised her voice and roared. "By all the heroes and saints that ever resided in the realm of this earth, in their name, I tell you to rise up."

The marionette did rise up slowly, lengthwise, and held its position in loose air. Zasu had done it. She had commanded. The doll had obeyed. Zasu bowed to P.J. She smiled at him, accepting his praise.

"It's all in the mind, you see, concentrating, believing, willing it to happen." And then they were interrupted by Amm, who came into the room and exposed Zasu's trick. It was done with wires. It was fake.

"You must not be tricked with false magic.", Amm warned.

When Harry came, he brought his Ouija board, or 'spirit board'. He would bring it out after dark when the adults were sleeping.

P.J. and Harry Dunne played cards in his room. They told each other stories and one was about Zasu making her marionette rise up off the floor and lie in a supine position, mid- air. He didn't tell him it was only a wire-trick. He wanted to scare his friend. It was fun to be scared when you had a friend over to spend the night. He told him about seeing his cousin's game of Mandrake the Magician in his room. Naturally, he wanted to show it to him, so the boys went downstairs, into the office, took the key to Will's room out of the drawer and went upstairs. Everyone else was sleeping. P.J. opened Will's door and it was too dark to see the game. They agreed to come back with a flashlight.

When Harry brought out the Ouija board he asked the question, "Should P.J. have the Mandrake Kit for his own use?" He moved the planchette either by purpose or will. The Ouija board said yes.

"It said you're supposed to have it. Let's go get it.", Harry announced. P.J. got the flashlight out of his drawer and they crossed the hall, unlocked the door to Will's room and slid the game out of its place on the shelf. They hurried out, taking it with them, locking the door behind. P.J. sat on the floor. He held the game. It felt weird and he did not feel well. He stole from the dead. The board had coerced him into stealing from the dead. What other terrible things could it make him do?

"Hey", said Harry. "I've had it since last Christmas, and it's never brought bad spirits on me. But if you feel that way, let's put it back where it was."

"No. I'm not going back in there, but I need to take the door key back downstairs before my sister finds it missing. Come on." He pushed the Mandrake set under his bed, the Ouija board with it. They tiptoed downstairs. Once the key was back in the desk, they felt safe again. But there were noises out the back door, coming from the alley.

"Check it out.", said Harry.

They opened the backdoor quietly, hoping it would not squeak. There was a screen door with a hook on it, that was secure. It was pitch dark, and someone had broken the light globe again. The boys placed their faces against the screen to peer out. They saw shadows of men out there, tramps off the boxcars. There looked to be three of them, bunched together tightly in a corner.

Suddenly, another face appeared against the screen. Mouth gaping open, glaring eyeballs within an inch of Harry's. Who yelled bloody murder, jumping backwards, tripping over P.J.'s knees, as he was trying to get up and out of there.

'No worse than me.", P.J. confessed P.J., later. "I steal magic sets from the dead. They steal food from the living."

It was not hard for Amm to hear them, because he had been alerted already, coming out on the balcony. He stood there looking down, as the clouds passed over the moon, then left it bright, shiny, and brilliant again. He could see three figures below. Tramps off the train. Up to no good.

Amm thew out his arms toward the night sky. He was powerful in his thrust. There was a generous wind in the air. It was thick. It would carry his weapon downward, with speed. He lassoed all three of them the first time he tried. One rope cast tied them together, those who would hide in the darkness, and frighten little children.

The nightwatchman, Early Watson, arrived at that moment, saw the spectacle of the three men, tied, scrambling to get untethered. He saw the two little ones inside the back door of the building, noses pressed against the screen. He eyeballed them. They screamed and ran.

The alleyway was empty once again after the nightwatchman untied the three hobos and sent them on their way out of town. There was no evidence the incident had ever taken place.

Amm didn't stay on the balcony to watch. He knew already, what would happen. Early Watson would come by on his rounds, find them, and turn them loose. Those three would bypass Grand Saline next time they jumped a train.

   He went downstairs to lock the back door. The screen door was still latched. No one had gotten in. He did walk through the rooms and found everything intact. All the doors and windows were secure.

   Upstairs, he looked in on P.J.'s room and both boys had their heads covered with quilts. They did not make a peep when Amm took the games from under the bed. They would sleep now. He went to his and Zasu's room and found her awake. She was ruffling through a magazine. She could not sleep.

"There are too many noises outside tonight.", she told Amm. "Did you find the boys well?"

"I don't think they will get out of their beds the rest of the night.", said her husband, Amm.

The next morning both the Mandrake game and the Ouija board were gone from under the bed.

"They disappeared.", said Harry. "I'll bet the Ouija board had enough power to make the Mandrake game disappear."

CHAPTER 9

The boys were playing, wrestling, on the floor in the dining room, where they were not supposed to play. Harry was on top; had P.J. pinned against the floor, good-naturedly, when something caught the sunlight from the front window. It came from underneath the credenza. The object hung loose. It had been taped to the wooden bottom. P.J. reached his arm through the narrow opening. It was a coin.

It was a gold color and immediately P.J. knew it would be an ideal decoration for the front of his turban. He put it in his pocket and continued to wrestle with his friend Harry Dunne. Enough with letting him win, he gave the boy a hard enough push that knocked Harry over and into the window. He hit his head and glass shattered. The yells of P.J. brought Amm immediately. Who saw what was happening. He yanked the white linen cloth off the nearest table and wrapped the boy, mostly his bleeding head, into the cloth. The boy was crying and so was P.J. Amm acted quickly and wasting not one second, proceeded to carry the tablecloth wrapped Harry across the street to Dr. Garland's office. It was upstairs, inside the drug store. The entourage of the family who were alerted, ran behind Amm, who was taking great strides. Dr. Garland received the boy quickly and his nurse got everything ready for the skilled hands that would stop the bleeding and decide whether stitches were needed.

"Go get his father.", Dr. told anyone who was listening. "And get everybody else out of here."

"I'll go. I know where he is.", volunteered P.J. Naturally Amm was far ahead of him and P.J. caught up as they both entered through the door of his business, which was only around the corner and across the street from the Grand Theatre.

Mr. Dunne was busy selling an expensive lawn mower to a customer.

"Go play, boy.", he said, with P.J. insisting he hear him, that his son was hurt, and he needed to come. He shoved P.J. slightly.

Before anyone could say, 'Jack Roberson', Amm had lifted Mr. Dunne, thrown him over his shoulder, turning him upside down.

He was hanging head-first looking perhaps at the change on the floor that fell out of his pocket. Riding the able shoulders of Amm and bobbing up and down, it didn't take two minutes to get the father to the doctor's office and at the side of his son, Harry Dunne. By then, the boy's head was shaven in a long strip at the top of his head, from front to back. He watched as the agile and delicate fingers of Dr. Garland took stitches. Harry was wide awake, in fair spirits considering the situation, and felt no pain. He met the eyes of his father and said, "I'm sorry, Dad. The window got in my way."

Later, Harry was lying on the bed in Dr. Garland's anti-room, resting a while before being taken home. P.J. was allowed to come in. He was frantic by then and wanted to see with his own eyes that his friend was okay. He felt responsible for the accident.

He said to Harry Dunne, "We are twins. We both have white head coverings."

Later when the bandages were removed, the two boys agreed that Harry would be an authentic Oliver Warbucks, with his shaved head that made him appear to be bald like the comic strip character, Daddy (Oliver) Warbucks, who had to go fight a war, leaving Little Orphan Annie in the hands of a protector, one hero, Punjab, a Pakistani Indian.

In the weeks following, they were a pair, Punjab and Daddy Warbucks. As yet, they had not named a Little Orphan Annie. But Harry's little sister, Deane Dunne, was vying for the position. She still allowed she could furnish the dog, as 'Sandy'.

When the glass was repaired in the dining room of the Snow Hotel, it was a different type. One could see out, but the outsiders could not see in, the diners eating their meal. That would be an improvement, all agreed. Just the one pane was replaced. It went the length across the bottom half of the front windows.

CHAPTER 10

The men of the fire department, including Tom Birdwell, were sponsoring their annual tomato festival, with boxing matches they held every year at the baseball field in Grand Saline. They brought in mostly black fighters from Terrell, Tyler, and Canton, Texas. Anyone could make bets on who would win. Folks were invited to put on the gloves. There were always takers. In conjunction with the matches, they would have a street dance on the town square, and fiddlers would come to town, the best ones from Athens, where they had regular dances on Saturday nights.

The Grand Saline fire department had a contract with the 'Bob Hurst Carnival' who had come to town each of the previous five years for the annual tomato festival.

    When they found the carnival had not finished setting up, had, in fact, moved on in the middle of the night before one tent had been raised, they naturally checked as to why. Learning that the Indian, Amm, who was running the Hotel Snow, had sent them off, the town men were not pleased at all.

    Why, he was an outsider, who came to town uninvited. He had no authority to cancel the carnival or anything else. The men of the fire department went to city hall and complained. They were told to bring them more information and make a formal complaint. That would take too long. So, they decided to pay the people at the Snow Hotel a little visit. They would go together and talk with this Mr. Amm, who was interfering in their plans.

They stood there, six of them, two firemen, the rest businessmen and organization representatives, all of them intimate friends to each other. No one wanted to be first to knock on the door. Each had lost his nerve and passed the buck to another to 'do something'.

The face of Amm met their stares of those men peering through the dining room glass windows. They jumped back, stunned for a moment in time. He appeared to have no body below his waist. His top half appeared to be floating in air. His lower half was shielded by the new portion of glass which would not allow them to see below Amm's waist. There was not one of them whose hair did not stand on end, seeing Amm, or rather his top half, his face against the window staring at them, his eyes, black and penetrating. But at that very moment, Amm was standing behind the group of men. They turned and he was there... among them, outside. How could that be? The men were all speechless, except the one who asked how he got out there that fast.

Bill Bates explained that they must have been looking at his reflection in the window from where he must have been standing all the while.

To which someone asked then, why couldn't they see their own reflections in the windows? They could not. They agreed the sun must have changed its position.

"See here, Mr. Amm." Alex Bryant said, "We have a bone to pick with you. It is important that you understand that this town was working well enough, with our traditions, before you came into it, forcing your foreign influences upon our residents."

"Now Alex", suggested Stan Hutchins, "You can get more with honey than with vinegar. I'm sure we can work this out peacefully with Mr. Amm, here."

He took over. "You see, that carnival setting up on the outskirts of town was part of our annual festival we have here in Grand Saline." He explained the entertainment, the boxing matches that benefit the Fire Department, and the Saturday night fiddling contest as well.

"Word is, you did something to scare the carnival people off. By doing so, you upset our apple cart. Do you understand Mr. Amm?"

Ben Brown piped in. "Tell him he's not welcome in this town. He's not one of ours. We don't like it. We don't like his kind."

Ben Baker spoke up. "We are all gentlemen here. It is not necessary to call names, nor to get physical," He got up into the face of Amm. "Not unless we have to, of course.", he threatened. "We do have a question though, we'd be glad to know the answer and that is why did you send them away, and what did you say to them? We'd like to apologize and get them back."

"Let's take him to them. Make him apologize to them directly. They'll come on back. We'll have our carnival, our festival, our boxing matches, our dancing in the streets."

Everyone had something to say, then. As they bickered amongst themselves, Amm disappeared. Without a word, he was gone.

"Where did he go?", they asked each another. They sputtered, peered into the glass window, and seeing no one, they disbursed; going their separate ways, wondering what had just happened.

CHAPTER 11

P. J. still had the coin. He had rubbed it all during the time his buddy, Harry, was getting sewn up. Perhaps it held good luck, because he wished, and prayed for his new friend, Harry Dunne, to make it. There had been a lot of blood. Now it was all over. He now fondled the gold coin and again fancied it atop his turban, a fine accent to his Punjab outfit. He asked Zasu if she could attach it to his turban. She thought it was from a box of Crackerjacks and told him she would make a tatted bezel for it. Within the bezel the coin lost most of its luster, sewed into the front of the turban. But it didn't take long for Marilyn to take notice of the 'jewel'.

"Where did you get that?", she asked P.J. (she, like everyone else used the short initials instead of the name 'Punjab', in conversation). He explained and immediately Marilyn knew it was the hundred- dollar payment for her grandfather's cotton he sold in Louisiana a generation earlier. She claimed it for her own since it was in the credenza she was to inherit.

"I didn't know anything about that.", P.J. said, through tears. He really liked the jewel in his turban. Marilyn admitted that neither the credenza nor the coin was hers...not yet. It belonged to her uncle, who was very much alive, and in another country.

"But it's not yours either, P.J." She took scissors and clipped off the bezel that held the coin. They would go the next morning to the bank and ask Mr. Keats if they should leave it there for safekeeping.

She brought it in; took P.J. with her. She went directly to Mr. Keats' desk and stood there, holding her tied-up handkerchief, with the coin inside. When he opened it a whiff of cologne drifted upward. Her personal scent, it was lilac.

Mr. Keats looked at the coin then, through a magnifying glass. He suggested they go across the street together, to the jewelers to get it appraised.

"What is its value...I mean for the insurance.", asked Keats.

"It is gold. It would be the current price of gold, as content. It would have increased in value of course. The condition is to be considered. Would you like a formal appraisal of the coin?", the jeweler asked.

"We'll be taking it with us. Thank you.", said Marilyn Snow.

Back at the bank, Keats insisted they keep it. He was the 'caretaker' of Mr. William Snow's financial assets and considered the gold coin a part of those.

"I only asked for your advice.", she said. Her voice was chilly. "That doesn't mean I have to take it. I will ask my father. The coin belonged to his father as well."

"I can't let you leave with it. I'm sorry."

When Marilyn and P.J. left, without the coin, Marilyn decided never to speak to Mr. Keats again. She was glad she had declined his invitation to go to the boxing matches on Saturday. He planned to fight. To her, that seemed ridiculous.

She remembered saying to him, "You? Fight?"

"And why not?" He wanted to take off his coat and tie, and shirt, and show her his well-developed muscles. Right there on Main Street, where they stood together. So what if everyone else saw. He was proud of his physique. Wearing glasses made him look like a banker. Boxing shorts would make him look like a contender.

P.J. decided he didn't like Mr. Keats for keeping the coin he had found under the credenza.

CHAPTER 12

Amm thought bicycling so soon after Harry's accident was not wise, so asked the two boys if he could serve them as 'The Asp' to chauffeur them around town on such a fine morning.

"There will be no climbing trees or wrestling matches, only a pleasant sack lunch at the town park." He would be teaching them some tricks they would enjoy.

"Magic tricks?" They became excited.

"Wait and see. You might find what I have to show you of value under certain circumstances in the future. One might see them as tricks. I consider them skills."

The boys are seated in the back seat. P.J. and Harry wear short pants and tee shirts, with tennis shoes. Harry still wears his bandage. He has seen his shaven head and stitches in the mirror and enjoys looking the part of Daddy Warbucks. His best friend, P.J. will be his bodyguard, as in the comic strip, 'Little Orphan Annie' in future games they will play. 'The Asp', Daddy Warbucks' chauffeur, is acting his part this very day, driving the automobile that will take them to the park.

   In the trunk are ropes. New ropes because the three hobos he lassoed in the alley, managed to get away with his regular ropes. These are shorter, and lighter and will be just right to teach the boys how to tie and toss a lasso.

   When they got to the park the boys had energy to spend. They sat at the picnic table, pouting a bit; sighing; wishing they could run and play, chin the bars, climb the trees, and wrestle. Amm would not allow them to chance Harry tearing his stitches.

It was time for Amm to illuminate them. He asked for their attention. Because they respected Amm's wisdom they listened.

"It is what you make it to be. Imagination is the key. The master key." He began speaking in a soft monotone.

"In front of you is the barren field. The grass has long been worn down, by many hooves. Soldiers have passed through, on their way to great battles. There will be more battles and more soldiers. At this moment in time, it is empty. You are relaxing and resting. When you open them, the quietness has been interrupted. The dust is kicking up in the distance. Hear the hooves tearing up ground. A vengeful enemy is approaching. A ram's horn announces their arrival.

   As you watch the noon sun pass over, it is unclear what or who is charging across the fields. It could be powerful soldiers, riding the finest horses that Kings' money can buy. An army, decked in silver armor, their swords out, coming to challenge you to the biggest, most dangerous battle of the century. You will have to fight them. You may not win. You may be facing death. But you will fight to the finish with honor."

   Amm stopped. He could tell both were alert to that possibility. Hadn't Harry got his head cut open, wrestling to see who could win that fight? That was only a game, they reasoned, with terrible consequences.

   "I tell you, you don't have to play that game. Not today. There is an alternative. Where you already won. Concentrate hard. Are you concentrating? Open your eyes.

Look across the fields. Do you see the armored soldiers, without swords, their clothes torn off them, blood dripping? They are riding away from you. You have won the battle. It is over. You are exhausted and can rest. You are proud. Lay down your swords. Take up your spoils, Pin your medals on each other. And claim your right to rest awhile. With honor. You are great heroes. Which of these two games will you choose to play today?   If you are wise."

"It is kinda hot.", said Harry. He had not gotten his full strength back yet.

"Yeah", said P.J. "I'm sweating already. And I didn't bring my sword with me today." He leaned back on the table and stared at the sky. It was noon. The sun was passing over. He was blinded and could not see any soldiers attacking. He blinked his eyes again, this time hard, and saw the soldiers running away, through the oak trees in the park. They were squealing like piggies. That bunch of sissies.

   The rest of the afternoon Amm taught the boys how to lasso posts, poles, each other, and even Amm. Who brought out pencil and paper and drew diagrams and instructions on the hundred different ways to tie a secure knot in a rope.

   The afternoon drifted into early evening. The ladies would be waiting for them at 'home', in the Hotel Snow. And he must return Harry Dunne to his.

CHAPTER 13

   When they got back to the hotel, there had been several packages delivered. Marilyn said if all the future 'souvenirs' were that heavy, they had better leave them downstairs, rather than in Will's room.

"We could not carry the latest arrival upstairs. In fact, this one is staying down here. It's a wormwood table. I hope the beetles are gone out of it.", she said.

"I could start a stamp collection with all these packages. So many different countries.", said P.J.

"When Uncle and Aunt come home, they will let you have the foreign stamps, P.J. In the meantime, why don't you start inventorying the packages on a world map. I will buy you one and some map pegs. Would you like that?"

Thus it was that many-a-night, or rainy day would be spent cataloging the packages that arrived almost daily. They seemed to be growing in size, such as the table. This activity satisfied P.J. when he and his friend, Harry Dunne could not go outside and act out their 'Little Orphan Annie' escapades. They still didn't have an 'Annie' yet but didn't seem to need one. Because of the rain, it wasn't even fun when Amm chauffeured them around, as Punjab, Daddy Warbucks and 'the Asp'.

The tomato festival had been postponed because of the continual rain. The city fathers decided to combine that annual event with the Fourth of July holiday. Make it a colossal weekend. The weather began to improve.

This particular evening, before the festivities began, the four of the family sat on the balcony together, noting the decorations in the town. The Hotel Snow had not put any out because they were still considered 'in mourning'. However, they would participate in some of the activities.

Posters were put up everywhere except the Snow Hotel. But inside, P.J. had managed to get two posters to keep. One promoted "The Bob Hurst Shows'. He owned the traveling carnival. It was wild and colorful and had freaks and fantasy, and best of all, a magician who looked suspiciously like 'Mandrake'. At least he wore a top hat, a black cape with red lining and carried a cane that seemed to be lit up with sparklers. It was a fine poster.

The other poster was for the boxing matches and was not so professional. Mostly black and white, and all of them window card size. They showed photographs of black boxers, famous or infamous. Everyone wanted to be Joe Louis, the new Heavy-weight Champion of the World. The names were not familiar to P.J. or Harry. They didn't mind boxing, but preferred wrestling, and only for fun.

Marilyn, Zasu and Amm forbade them to go to the planned boxing matches. Even Mr. Keats told them it was going to be 'bloody bad'. He was going to be in it. P.J. didn't care much for Mr. Keats anyway...still sore about the gold coin. It wasn't right of him to keep the coin in his old bank when his sister wanted to bring it home.

It was July now and P.J. figured their vacation was half-over. It was going by so fast, he realized. They had to pack in a lot of fun and experiences before his aunt and uncle returned to reclaim the hotel.

The carnival would be one of them. He was especially interested in the sideshow called, 'Throw the Dwarf'. Marilyn did not know about that show at the carnival. But it was written on the poster. 'Throw The Dwarf'. Would it be a real dwarf person? What would they do? Throw him (or her) back and forth by the seat of the pants? Or by his head, like a bouncing ball?

It has to be a stuffed doll, decided P.J. Seemed carnivals used a lot of kinds of dolls, chalk dolls, rubber dolls, celluloid baby dolls and raggedy anns.

They could go to the parade, beginning at the Morton Salt House, that had been constructed for the 1924 Texas Centennial. It was built out of blocks of pure salt. It would be the first.

Little girls vied for the honor of being named the 'salt girl' of 1938. She would wear a crown and ride on a float, sitting on a throne. Those who came in second or third would ride with her, dressed in yellow dresses just like the one on the front of the Morton Salt box. After the floats there would be the local high school band, and automobiles carrying beauty queens of school classes.

Leading the parade would be the flag bearers, carrying the National flag, the State of Texas flag and the Grand Saline, High School banner. Men dressed like 'Uncle

Sam' would walk on 'tom walkers' (or rather walking stilts) that covered their pants' legs to make them look tall.

   Naturally, P.J. wanted some tom walkers and Amm agreed to help him make a pair. They could go to the lumber yard and have them saw off some timber to the right size to make him tall.

   "I want to be eight ft. tall like Punjab really is in the funny papers."

   "After the festival is over.", Amm told the boy.

   Other bands would follow, and more floats depicting the celebration of the fourth of July, Independence Day. Policemen on decorated motorcycles would ride in practiced procession, with some fancy turning and circling, and cowboys would ride prancing horses, those being last.

There were many people on the streets, and a lot of motion and commotion. No one saw who broke the locks on the door to the club room at the Snow Hotel. No one saw the thieves go inside and carry out all the packages, including the wormwood table.

But Zazu, who always 'observed' before reacting, suggested that a certain truck, turning the corner of Frank Street on two wheels was carrying many of the same kind of packages that had been arriving at the hotel. In fact, the table, a part of the load, looked familiar. Once alerted, Amm was already on his way, with P.J. following. Good thing that Amm was late in returning the automobile to its garage at William Snow's residence. More and more he believed it should stay parked, when not in use, close to the hotel.

Amm and P.J. were in the Model A, but the truck had a head-start. Both spotted the thieves headed toward Highway 80. But how did they know about all the 'loot' they could steal from the Hotel Snow? It was no secret. Everyone in town was talking about all the treasures from foreign countries arriving each and every day. They marveled at the money being spent on, probably, frivolities.

When Amm was fairly close behind the truck, P.J. wanted to overtake them but was told to wait. They should follow closely behind them and block them in at the first opportunity. They would not get away with the thievery.

"Are you sure?", asked P.J.

"When they see the 'Detour' sign, they will have to turn around."

"What detour sign?", P.J. asked.

"That one.", Amm said, as he made an unexplained gesture with a few magic motions and words.

The truck carrying the stolen goods had to stop, back up and turn around, almost colliding with the Snow's car. The truck jerked and the driver gunned the motor and off they drove, only to find another 'Detour' sign blocking that street. And another one after that. By then, the thieves were turning around in circles, and recognized Punjab, all dressed up in his attire. The driver looked like a gangster, with his fedora hat. They reluctantly took the truckload of packages and furniture the only route that the detour signs allowed them, to the Hotel Snow. The two men even unloaded the truck and took the packages and table inside the club room of the hotel.

"Thank you.", said Amm.

"Thank you", said P.J.

The thieves were allowed to leave. P.J. remarked that one of them looked familiar. To which Amm replied he ought to.

"He delivers mail and packages to us most every day. He will be resigning in the morning."

Marilyn asked if they thought all the packages were accounted for. P.J. said he would check them against his world map where he had attached picks for that purpose. He asked for help, and Zasu volunteered. She looked at the first package and while she rarely raised her voice, she did this evening to P.J., calling out the country of origin.

"London, England…. tea set."

"Check.", said P.J.

"Marseilles, France… tea set."

"Check."

"Rome, Italy...tea set."

"Are they all tea sets? And how do you know without opening them?"

"I don't know. Marilyn just said the lady liked her tea, and collected tea sets.", said Zasu.

CHAPTER 14

The following day was July the fourth. There would be many festivities. 'The Adventures of Tom Sawyer' was being shown free of charge all day at the 'Grand Theatre'. The evening movie would change to 'The Marx Brother' Marilyn and Zasu would take P.J. to the matinee, to begin shortly after the parade finished. It would cheer him a little, since he was forbidden to attend the boxing matches at the baseball field with Amm, who intended to go watch.

   The' Grand' was packed, and P.J wanted to sit on the front row. They sat in the middle, as a compromise. Mrs. Dunne had brought Deane and Harry with her and sat down beside them.

   "Deane is going to open the show with a song.", the mother bragged and that was why she was wearing red, white and blue. Sure enough she excused herself with a cute bow, and in moments the projectionist shined his spotlight on the balcony banister where Deane now stood. She sang her patriotic song, Miss Kate Smith's 'God Bless America'. She had a healthy range, and the microphone blasted her voice, filling the theater with song. The patrons all stood with respect. Shortly, Deane came back to her seat and had her mother to move down one so she could sit by P.J. to watch the movie.

"I've been told this movie is very scary when the children go into the cave. Don't be surprised if I need your support. I may faint.", she told P.J.

"Don't count on it.", he told her.

The town knew how to celebrate and decorate, since their Texas Centennial, in 1924 had been such a success. The first salt palace they had built out of blocks made of pure salt still stood intact. Many visitors stopped in Grand Saline to see it. This year there would be many festivities. One was the boxing matches that P.J. was not allowed to watch. It might be bloody. The posters implied they might. One such poster starred a familiar Palooka Perry from Gladewater, Texas. Locals were pointing him out.

Meanwhile, at the baseball field, they were bringing in the fighters for the advertised matches. They were popular, coming from Terrell and Kaufman, Canton and Tyler. There were famous names from East Texas. There was the Texas Clipper, in the person of Leroy Ross from Canton and Willie Lee Johnson they called 'Cotton', from Tyler. Very popular was Knuckles Kelly, as well as 'The Klawhammer' from Kaufman. Rounding out the program would be Bluto Bruiser from Edgewood and Calvin Keats, (hometown challenger). Two subs were Bull Branigan and Killer Keller from Wills Point and Forney.

Only a month before, in June 1938, the amazing Joe Louis, from Alabama, had won the World Heavy-weight Championship in the first round, from Max Schmeling from Germany. Because of the upheaval there, with the rise of Hitler, the German was someone who must be annihilated, in the eyes of Americans, preferably by an American. That man was Joe Louis. He became instantly famous and every black fighter in the USA wanted to be the next Joe Louis.

Every year for the past five years, the Grand Saline Fire Department sponsored the tomato festival. Bob Hurst brought his carnival of five rides with five shows and five concessions to town. Also, the boxing matches became a huge part of the weekend. This year, 1938, was extra special because of the sensational Joe Louis, the new Heavy-weight Champion of the World. He was called, 'The Black Bomber' and was from Alabama. All the challengers who came to the matches were black except for one.

That one lived in Grand Saline. He was Mr. Keats, from the First State Bank. Under his reserved demeanor and clothing, he was an athlete. With his amazing physique he would surprise many in Grand Saline, who considered him strictly a banker. He chose the name, 'The Grand Saline Indian Fighter', and wore black trunks with a burnt orange stripe down each side, the colors of the local school.

He could have worn an Indian headdress of feathers and painted his face as a warrior, but chose instead, to simply wear a football helmet that said, 'G.S. Indians', and he would have all the support of the people in town. Everyone loved the football team. At first few recognized him. Then the buzzing started. "He's the banker man."

Amm came to watch. He blended in with the crowd, men, women, and children alike. He did not want to bring attention to himself. He had seen the buckets of rotten tomatoes being brought in, their intention evident. Every year there was some throwing of tomatoes at the challenger of the one they laid bets on. Amm positioned himself. He would have some fun. When the first tomato was propelled, he flattened his palm and placed it in its path, returning it to the pitcher. With speed faster than a blink of an eye, it splattered on that one's perfectly white shirt. Who was baffled. Do tomatoes ricochet?

When another came, Amm put out his palm again and that tomato proved tomatoes are unpredictable, when Amm is around to 'observe' and then react. Two white shirts showed themselves to one another and the wearers suspected each other.

It was not hard for Amm to keep up with the tomatoes being thrown at the fighters, however when the spectators started throwing them at each other, it became a brawl.

The sponsors, the fire fighters, had their trucks on the spot. They began unrolling a hose and someone looked for the nearest fire hydrant. Watering down those who had the most tomato sauce on them first, there were many who just wanted to get in on the fun. There was screaming, but mostly laughter. They were careful no children got in the way. Fortunately, K Wolens department store brought out large white towels and brand-new white shirts for the tomato splashed spectators. It was good publicity. The owner of Darby's department store wished he had thought of that. But they would have their moment in the sun presenting the championship belt with buckle to the winner of today's boxing matches, this 4th. of July festival.

The design on the buckle was no less than the Little Salt Girl with her blue and yellow box of pouring Morton salt.

Earlier, the sponsors, the fire department had come roaring onto the baseball field, sirens blaring, for the introduction of six fighters. There were cheerleaders following, each carrying a sign with a name of one of the boxers. The girls jumped and bounced and did cartwheels. They did cheers as each contender was introduced:

One wore a royal blue cape, known as the Klawhammer from Kaufman, Texas. He was standing on the running board, waving his hammer at bystanders. Then there was Bluto Bruiser, Hatchett Harry, Butch 'Red' Barron, and the Dallas Destructor. Then, the mayor himself rode in with the featured fighters, in a 1938 Deluxe Ford convertible. It was bright shiny red. The Texas Clipper and Cotton Johnson stepped out, as the cheers and boos commenced.

Last of all there was Mr. Keats, imitating the rest of them, with the fancy footwork, and showing off his biceps. Making a big deal out of putting on his football helmet, the home towners whistled, cheered and clapped for him, and for the team he represented, the Grand Saline Indians. Then the tomato melee began. After that it was evident the boxing ring was not fit for the boxers to fight. They would slip and slide and it would become a 'tomato mud fight'.

The Klawhammer pulled up one post of the ring. Three more fighters pulled up the others. Amm saw what they intended, and he gathered the ropes.

Quite a sight to see hanging on to the firetruck, the boxers, all wearing colorful trunks and expressionistic make-up, being hauled, with the firefighters to a dryer spot on the baseball field to perform their matches. Down the field they went, cheerleaders and spectators following, good humoredly. They did not want to miss a single minute of excitement.

The Klawhammer (he had a clawhammer handy as a prop for his costume) dramatically presented his weapon to set the posts, done in a moment's time, and Amm lassoed each of the four posts with the ropes and pulled them tight, and 'Bingo', there was a brand new and dry boxing ring. They would begin, with a sound of the Grand Saline High School band cymbals instead of a gong.

"Come out shaking hands.", ordered the referee.

First there would be two. Then two more, Then the winners of those two fights would fight the winner of the third and fourth fight. The finale would be against the last two standing. Bets were heavy. Money was exchanged readily, most likely family savings and food money for the coming week.
But they were having fun.

At one point, when Demolition Dallas threw Bluto Bruiser over the ropes, and drove himself through the ropes he was about to swing one more punch when a woman of broad girth, swung her purse at him and bopped him good. She looked familiar to Amm. And then he watched to see if she took her specialty out of her purse and smashed him an old-fashioned pie-in-the-face, he would know then it was, indeed, Ms. Bertha, from the Rayborne Café.

   The Grand Saline Indian, also known inside the First State Bank, as Mr. Keats, was the last man standing. He would, in the circles of boxing aficionados be known as the Grand Saline Indian Fighter.

   The K Wolens department store and the Grand Saline Firefighters cleaned them up, but Mr. Calvin Keats cleaned them out. He won a fortune betting on himself.

   Mr. Keats was cheered by all. Since he did not spill any blood, and no one was taken out on a stretcher there were those who opined,

"He's no Joe Louis. The Black Bomber would have taken all of them at the same time in one round."

CHAPTER 15

Back at the Grand Theatre, Mrs. Dunne was complimented on her daughter's performance.

She invited Marilyn to come to Rhodesburg the following week to attend the 'Playhouse Theatre's performance of 'Tootsie's Last Adventure.' Deane had a formidable role.

At that moment the manager approached them to compliment Deane and Mrs. Dunne. Who asked him, "Have you met Miss Snow?", and introduced Marilyn Snow to Neely Berry. That was most likely the real reason Neely, the manager came over...to meet that beautiful woman everyone was talking about who was occupying the Hotel

Snow for the summer. He shook hands with her and suggested refreshment for the children.

   Mrs. Dunne spoke first.

   "Why did you have the balcony all roped off today, of all days? All these kids could have gone up there and we would have had more breathing room down here.

   Neely did not let her off so easily, with her incessant complaints, she with her 'Playhouse Actors' organization.

   "But Mrs. Dunne. You know why the balcony is closed. We've had too many complaints about the misbehavior up there, unsupervised, and the noise and scuffling. Why, someone might have knocked your daughter off the balcony even as she sang those high notes."

Neely remembered Mrs Dunne's name being at the top of the list of complainants.

She left in short order. There stood only Marilyn, P.J. and Zasu.

"I gather I'm not invited to the Playhouse performance next week to see her daughter steal the show.", said Zasu. She laughed at being ignored entirely all afternoon by Mrs. Dunne. She apparently didn't exist in that woman's limited world.

Neely told her she did not have to be invited. Just needed to buy a ticket. "In fact, I'd love for all of you to be my guests." He meant it, smiling at each of them, lingering upon Marilyn a moment to meet her eyes that said yes.

So did she.

CHAPTER 16

With P.J. tugging on the sleeve of his sister, to go straight to the carnival grounds, she informed him they would go to the hotel, meet up with Amm, and eat something, then go to the carnival, but only for an hour or two.

"Remember", she said, "Our house is in mourning. You must behave. Is Harry joining us?"

"He'll be there. He's probably there now, looking for me. Let's not keep him waiting."

"I would imagine Mrs. Dunne will make him eat something as well. With his head shaven like Daddy Warbucks, they might put him in the freak show, along with you in your Punjab suit. Why don't you dress normal this evening?", she laughed. "If you will, I'll give you an extra quarter to spend at the carnival."

Amm was waiting at home, full of stories to tell about the tomatoes vs. fighters' boxing matches. He had P.J. laughing heartily as they all ate sandwiches.

"Will you show me how to detour those tomatoes? You're sure good at detouring things; Aunt Helen's packages coming back here after being stolen, and now rotten tomatoes getting thrown back at people. Say, did you help any one of the boxers win or lose?"

"That would have been wrong, P.J."

"Yeah. It wouldn't be fun to win by rook or crook. I wondered how Mr. Keats won over all those famous boxers. He's such a lightweight."

"I wish you could have seen him." Amm was talking at Marilyn. "He is well-built, toned, most certainly trained. He covers it all up, at the bank, where he must act professional to be taken seriously. We are not always what we seem. Today he was different. I do wish you could have been there to see him."

"I'm sure he will tell us all about it.", said Marilyn. "Let's go to the carnival now and get back early. It's already been a long day." She had promised to meet Keats there later. It was that time.

CHAPTER 17

Harry was waiting at the makeshift gate of the carnival. He had his sister with him.

"Oh no, why'd he have to bring her?" Deane Dunne was there with him. She didn't wear a costume of Orphan Annie (was there ever a costume for her?) but nevertheless she did look a little like the comic strip orphan girl, with her orangish hair.

"Hi P.J.", she said, girlishly. She had a crush on him. They hurried off, the three of them, with Marilyn and Zasu sounding safety warnings their way.

"The girl will slow them down, perhaps." said Zasu.

Amm remarked that they will run faster just to lose her, a girl. And one that clearly wanted him for a boyfriend.

They laughed. And then there stood Mr. Keats.

"What is his first name anyway?", asked Amm.

"It just says, "C.C. Keats" on his desk at the bank.", said Marilyn as she greeted him, boxing champion of the 1938 Fourth of July Festival, in conjunction with the annual tomato festival. Local hero of the day.

"I heard you won everything, all kit and caboodle", said Marilyn. She was polite. Not quite as angry with him as she was, over the gold coin. "You didn't wear your Championship belt?"

"That thing is so heavy it would drag my pants down to my knees.", he said.

"I would not want that to happen." She laughed. He was shy, with his new friends. With Marilyn.

I want you on that merry-go-round, getting dizzy enough to fall into my arms. I want you on that Ferris wheel, hanging onto me for dear life. I want your fortune told that you are going to marry me.

Charles Calvin Keats, did not say those things out loud. It was evident; all over his face, in his eyes, in his actions as he paired off with Marilyn Snow that he wanted to say them.

Zasu and Amm went their own way, perhaps to catch up with the boys followed by another who was in love, tonight, in a carnival of lights, mystery, and excitement. That would be Deane Dunne.

P.J., Harry and Deane rode the five rides. They did not see the dancing girls on stage. Boring. They did see every freak show including the midgets, or dwarfs.

Sure enough no one was throwing dwarfs. It was a trick, where the little people, also called midgets, sat, took hold of their toes and rolled themselves up in a tight ball. They were gently pushed forward, rolling themselves across the floor and then were gently pushed back to where they were. Back and forth they rolled, and the spectators, among them, P.J. and Harry realized they had been bamboozled.

The boys and Deane were repulsed by the fat lady, and enthralled with the tallest pony in the world They knew the 'pickled baby in the jar' was one of the celluloid dolls. Could even see the joints where the rubber band fastened arms and legs to the body. They tossed pennies in a can, missing every one, and there met up with Marilyn and Zasu with Amm and Keats.

"What is that dripping all over your clothes?"

Marilyn handed them more pennies to throw into tin cans set up behind the booth.

"It's a fish in a bag of water. I'm holding it for P.J.", said Deane. She held it up proudly.

Keats wanted to win something for Marilyn.

Too quickly he pulled out a coin from his pocket and it sparkled in Amm's eyes, alerting him that it was not copper like a penny. It was gold. He should be throwing copper pennies into the tin cans. As Keats threw the coin, Amm had sneaked under the booth, and intervened into the path of the coin. Quickly he tilted the tin can, causing it to clink into the air and he caught it. It was gold. It was the golden coin that was paid, a generation ago, to one farmer from Big Sandy, Texas, for a load of cotton. It had been passed to William Layfayette Snow, who was now vacationing in a foreign country. Keats realized what he had done.

"I thought..."

Marilyn was furious. "You had the gold coin in your pocket? Not in your bank vault? I trusted the bank. I trusted you."

"I took it to the jewelers for an appraisal. The bank was closed by the time I returned. It was for the long July 4th. holiday."

Amm reached for Keats' left ear and pretended to take the coin out, to hand it to him, and to get him out of trouble.

"Look here. How'd that get in your ear?" Amm said. It was not funny and did not appease Marilyn, who abruptly insisted he leave her presence, and without the coin.

"I'm sorry.", he said to her. His apology was sincere. He did leave the carnival grounds but took the gold coin with him. It would be in the First State Bank's possession when the door opened for business on Monday.

It was time for all of them to go home. Home was, for the time being, the Snow Hotel.

CHAPTER 18

When the manager from the Grand Theatre, Neely, came to the hotel to pick up

Marilyn, he had almost forgotten he had invited the kid, too, and their keeper, Zasu. He was gallant, though, and polite. He intended to make an impression on this woman, Marilyn Snow, who just last week had entered his life.

"Glad we brought chairs out here. The ground is wet.", Neely told his guests, Marilyn, and Zasu, who brought P.J. to play with Harry Dunne. Who had to come with his mother to watch his sister, Deane act her part in the play, 'Toosie's Last Adventure".

They arrived at Rhodesburg, also known locally, as Poletown, right out of the city limits of Grand Saline, where, once a month, the Playhouse Actors' Guild, a club of performers, put on a show for the public. Tonight, it was a typical love story, 'Boy Meets Girl, Boy loses Girl, Boy gets girl back.' Always a popular storyline, and in this instance two children had strong roles to play, and P.J.'s friend's sister, Deane Dunne, had several lines and performed several stunts of consequence. One was a scene where she had to be saved after almost falling off a balcony. She was hanging by one hand. Her father, in the play, did save her.

"My darling girl.", he said, and showered her with make-believe kisses. The End.

The boys, P.J. and Harry did not watch the play with their elders. They were also hanging, from limbs of trees. watching (maybe) from a distance. Realizing the show was over, they came running back to the chairs, all gone now, except those Marilyn, Zasu and Neely still occupied. Neely did not want the evening to end, it seemed.

" These chairs out here in the night air, watching an outdoor play gives me an idea. I would like to have your input. Yours as well, Zasu. ", began Neely.

"Can we go play some more?", the boys asked, seeing Mrs. Dunne bringing Deane their way. Not waiting for an answer, they ran.

Neely's idea was to take the chairs from the balcony at the Grand Theatre and donate them to the Playhouse Actors' Guild for their outside performances. He said there were two dozen but welded together in two separate rows. He doubted whether he could get them off the balcony, onto the ground floor and out the door unless he took them apart in sections. What did they think? He continued.

"I get so many complaints about that balcony, 'Keep it open, rope it off, adults only, children only, make it a room for mothers nursing their babies (that's a good one)." He laughed. "They say there's too much misconduct with no supervision up there. Even the projectionist complains he can't hear the movie he's showing on the screen and no one else can either."

"I think that is a wonderful idea, Neely, to donate the chairs to our performers. I will suggest that to them at the next meeting we have.", said Mrs. Dunne, who interjected without being asked. Her daughter, Deane, was looking around for the boys, for accolades perhaps.

Neely told her it was simply an idea still in the thinking process, and not to approach the committee about it yet. They gathered their folding chairs and left in one group, the boys catching up, with Deane in their midst, and heading for their separate cars.

Neely would be bringing up the subject of 'balcony chairs' again, but not in the presence of Mrs. Dunne. She butted in when she wasn't asked an opinion. He asked Marilyn if they might go out for dinner. He had much rather see Marilyn alone, next time. If he could swing it.

CHAPTER 19

Neely Berry approached the owners, the Elk brothers, about removing the balcony chairs, perhaps donating them to the Playhouse Actors' Guild in Grand Saline. The Civic Club had signed a petition at the suggestion of Mrs. Dunne. Most adults wanted the balcony closed. So did the projectionist. He had threatened to quit. Too much hassle up there with the noisy kids arguing with the adults. Those downstairs complained about getting popcorn dumped on their heads and drinks. Occasionally, someone did fall from up there.

"We're tired of hearing about it. Get 'em out of there.", was the unexpected answer from the owners. Neely expected a bigger argument.

"How?", he asked.

"Simple. Call the people who put em' in there.", was the answer. "Tell 'em to come and take 'em out."

However, it was not that simple. The professionals who arrived, with their truck that would transport the chairs to Rhodesburg, their new home, brought their equipment, mainly pliers and screwdrivers, not expecting so much 'help' from Grand Saline spectators. School was out and every kid in town was there, running in and out of the theatre. Climbing the balcony stairs and being turned back. They needed a policeman to guard the doors. The nightwatchman was brought in and was able to keep the kids outside. All except one, Deane Dunne on her roller skates no less. She took them off and her feet on the carpet of the stairs to the balcony were so light, she was able to sneak into the room where the men were working to unhinge the chairs, separate them and lift them to an assembly line, formed from the exit door to underneath the balcony. There was a problem between that gap, those lifting them over the balcony rails, and those taking hold, to pass them along.

"Bridge the gap.", said P.J. "With my tom-walkers I can do that." He grabbed his bike and rode as fast as he could, back to the hotel to get them. They would made him eight foot tall. He could bridge the gap between those handing over the chairs and those taking hold of them to pass them down the assembly line to the waiting truck.

Deane Dunne relived, in her mind, her dramatic experience, singing 'God Bless America' from the edge of the balcony. She thought about that night. She also remembered acting in 'Once in Every Life' at Rhodesburg, where she dangled from a balcony, and was saved by her 'Daddy' who kissed her and called her, 'My Darling Girl'. She could re-enact that scene and P.J. would most certainly come save her. She felt sure of that. If not, someone else would. She saw the photographer with his camera. He came from the Grand Saline Sun. He would take her picture and put it in the newspaper and there would be all that publicity. She would get many movie star roles after this stunt. So as the action continued, she waited for the right moment.

P. J. had brought in his tom walkers to satisfy the break between those passing the chairs from the balcony to those receiving them, in the assembly line downstairs. He, being eight foot tall in tom walkers, he could pass one chair at a time over the balcony rail. How the boy expected to hold on to a theater chair and not fall off his tom walkers, was moot. He wanted to be in on the excitement. He wanted to be a hero.

But the adults in the room stopped him and told him to take his tom-walkers outside. To 'go play'. He became a hero anyway, when he saw Deane Dunne dangling from the balcony, shouting 'Save me.' He, on his tom walkers stood beneath her, only inches from her feet, being eight foot tall on stilts. He signaled her to drop a little ways and grab hold of his back and he would carry her the few steps she needed to be, for her mother to take over from there. The mother, Mrs. Dunne was none too happy with her daughter's spectacle.

She said to her, "They could see your underwear." The newspaper man got his story, with many action photos, including the little girl who fell from the balcony and was saved by an eight-foot young man (on stilts,), dressed up like a funny paper hero.

When all the chairs were loaded, there were remarks that they were torn in places, and sticky with years of dried-up chewing gum stuck on the bottoms and even coupons still attached that were given out as free drinks and popcorn if it was under your chair. That was during grand opening nine months previously. There were, installed then when the 'Grand' was brand new, 380 seats. The balcony that held twenty-four, was now empty, the carpet, once new, was now torn, pulled up, and tossed aside in a nasty heap.

"As is.", was the condition the 'Elks' owner set when he gave away the theatre chairs. Mrs. Dunne said she had not considered the chairs would be in such poor condition and repairs were not in their budget. She would have to ask her Playhouse Actors Guild committee if they would accept the chairs...in their current condition.

"Are you kidding?", Neely Berry was speechless. The chairs were already loaded and ready to be delivered to Rhodesburg.

Mrs. Dunne told them she could not take the responsibility, knowing they were in such poor condition.

"They just need a little soap and water.", said Neely.

"I thought they were nicer when you asked me to take them off your hands. They are dirty.", she said. "But I will make some calls in the morning and ask around if anybody wants them. But now, I have to get my child home for her dinner."

Those who remained were dumb struck.

There were two vehicles on the street downtown, that night. Both parked. But not together, nor deserted. Early Watson would keep an eye on the Elks' truck loaded with theatre chairs until the driver had his dinner at the M&M Hotel across from the picture show and slept a while upstairs in a hotel room. Amm kept watch on his employer's automobile parked in front of the Snow Hotel. The truckdrivers had brought an empty truck, filled it with two dozen chairs, and would now have to wait until morning to find out their destination...to Rhodesburg to their little theatre, which was just an abandoned church building, or somewhere else, maybe to the city dump.

Amm was talking with Early Watson, nightwatchman, trading stories for a while until most onlookers were gone on home, the excitement over. Then Amm drove his employer's automobile, the Model A Ford, back to William Snow's home, safe in its garage. Then he walked back to the hotel, like he did every night.

Neely was being calmed by the beautiful Marilyn Snow, on her balcony overlooking the Morton Salt Evaporating Plant, with its 300 foot smokestack. They spent the rest of the evening getting to know each other better. They had a lot in common, and she liked his good humor, absent since Mrs. Dunne's refusal of the chairs. She changed the subject and told him about hers.

"I have some chairs also. Or will have. Fourteen of them. Not sixteen. But fourteen. The others are floating around out there somewhere. Or else some cowboys used them to break over the other cowboys' heads."

"What on earth are you talking about, Woman?" He was laughing by then. They talked about his and her chairs for a while and shared a generous slice of Ms. Bertha's blueberry pie she had sent up earlier. He asked her to marry him, and he would build her a house that warranted thirty-four chairs. She said that 24 theatre chairs and fourteen dining chairs added up to thirty-six, not thirty-four.

"You don't understand; two of them had sticky chewing gum stuck on the bottom. I had to throw those away." They both howled. It was both silly and funny. So were they.

Amm and Zasu checked their calendar, marking off the remaining days of the summer, at least the time they would spend in the town of Grand Saline, in the hotel named "Snow" and with the many people who lived in a town such as this. Then they talked of other things. They both would have liked to accompany the Snows to their own home country where they were born and shortly after, brought to the United States. The Snow's latest letter was shared with everyone, describing in detail the beauty and wonder of the Arabian Sea. Punjab, Pakistan was in the northern part. They longed to go there one day and prayed that would happen.

The next morning, the truck pulled out early. Orders were to bring all the theatre chairs back to the manufacturing company for 'revamping'. The balcony would be used for presentations, and small receptions.

When the packages started arriving, the curiosity was strong. P.J. was cataloguing them according to the postage stamps and their origin. He visualized what was in each one, according to size, shape, and even smell. Because he did recognize that of the candied citrus and scented candles.

Zasu reasoned the heavy ones that were arriving further into the trip were probably bed linens, for friends who appreciate fine cotton goods from Punjab, Pakistan.

P.J. said, "Daddy has the best cotton anywhere around. We like our own cotton." After a moment he added, "I don't want any old bedsheets for presents."

"Don't expect toys, P.J. In fact, don't expect anything."

"I'd like a real magic carpet. They could send me one of those, and I could ride it over there to meet Uncle William and Aunt Helen. I could see what they're seeing. I could bring you back some real presents, not cotton sheets. I could bring you back some pink salt crystals to put in your bath water, Zasu. Wouldn't you like that?"

"Very much, P.J."

"I know all about Pakistan, thanks to 'Little Orphan Annie' comics.

"And Amm and me."

"But Zasu, you've never lived there. You've not sailed the Arabian Sea, climbed their stone mountains. You've never been through their caverns and caves. You've never ridden a camel or slept in the desert sand with one of them as your only companion. Never watched their Arabian sunsets with all those colors, yellow and orange, and red. Or been inside their Himalayan salt mines. They have salt mines, but not white like in our saltshakers we sprinkle on our food. Theirs is pink crystalline. It's called halite. Like what I'm going to bring you back when I go there."

Zasu said, "In your dreams, P.J. You can't hop, skip and jump yourself right into Pakistan."

"Oh, but I could if I had a magic carpet.", said P.J. The boy fell asleep then, perfectly content. He could dream, couldn't he?

When the living area that once was a club room for Grand Saline residents, was spilling over, with tables and chairs, chests and statues, even urns and pots, sent home from foreign countries it became burdensome, leaving no space in the living room to lie down or stretch out. P.J. lost his curiosity, except for the postage stamps on the packages he continued to catalogue.

CHAPTER 20

The summer sailed by. In no time at all, it was P.J.'s birthday. He was an August child, a Leo. There finally was a package for him. And it was, indeed, a magic carpet. It was yellow and green silk with gold and silver threads embroidered throughout. Jewels were embedded in the tassels on each of the ends. His family and friends were there for the grand opening of 'the gift'. And P.J. was ecstatic. He impulsively took Zasu's scissors and snipped off one of the tassels, asking her to attach it to his turban, where the golden coin had once been sewn on. She was shocked that he would cut off one of the tassels so suddenly. What if the magic carpet was forever grounded?

P.J. laughed. "Ah Ha. You do believe in its power then? Don't worry, it will fly with or without the tassels." He was decked out in white pants, white shirt, red and yellow cummerbund and turban that now sported the jeweled tassel from his own, truly magnificent magic carpet from Punjab, Pakistan. It was his birthday, and anything was possible. Marilyn was reading the engraved card that came with the gift.

"It is said that the Queen of Sheba had an alchemist to create a carpet of green and gold silk with precious jewels embedded in the fabric. She wanted to give it to King Solomon as a token of her love. The alchemist used a dye that held special powers, made from a clay that had magnetic properties. Since the earth is magnetic, the carpet had the ability to hover over earth hundreds of miles above it."

It had been the morning his father would be coming into town, bringing his cotton to the gin. He was to arrive early, be the first, so that he would win the bonus, and have his cotton on display on the town square, He would be important. He had dreamed of this day. But he had not arrived yet. He would not get the bonus or have his cotton on display. Someone else beat him to it. P.J. was very disappointed. He had awakened early and slipped out before daylight, running on foot to the Highway 80 intersection to watch for his daddy's arrival. Who had not come, even now. His cotton trucks were nowhere in sight when Amm came to get P.J. His birthday presents were waiting to be opened. His friends were there, to watch him blow out his thirteen candles.

   "I am a man. I am thirteen.", he was crying real tears. "My daddy is not here to see me become thirteen. And he didn't win the contest to be the first to bring in the cotton to be ginned in this county."

Amm reassured him that the traffic of all the trucks and wagons coming in, had slowed him down, but that he would be here.

"We can wait on the cake. There are cookies. And light the candles again later when your daddy arrives. But you must not make your friends wait any longer to see you open your gifts. They want to celebrate your birthday, but they want also to go watch the farmers bringing in their cotton. It's a grand day for all of them. They have the gin running constantly and the town is full of farmers waiting their turn. You don't want them to miss out on that. Do you? Come on, Punjab, this is the 'Asp' telling you to be strong. Be a leader. Save the day."

His back would be the chauffeured automobile to transport the thirteen-year-old to his birthday gathering, to open gifts, one of which was a genuine, authentic, magic carpet, waiting to fly him to the moon, or to the Arabian Sea.

CHAPTER 21

P.J. sat on top of seventy pounds of cotton, in one of his daddy's trucks, that hauled them to the gin. They were packed so tightly that no air could take an inch of space. Why haul air? He watched his daddy moving about. Who had no right to complain. He was late and would wait in line to have his load of cotton ginned, along with the dozens in his same position. There were only four people running the gin. They could only service a limited amount every hour. He knew he was at the end of the line…waiting. So much of that today. There was his son, who had been waiting all morning long, to get the first glimpse of his daddy driving his Model A automobile, his cotton trucks coming right along behind him, up the Highway 80 to town, to the gin. Not the nearest one to his farm, but the one where his family was waiting to come home, back to Big Sandy, after three months of living in Grand Saline, minding the Snow Hotel, while its owners, (his brother, William and wife Helen) went on their jaunt. They sailed from New York on a big ship, taking eleven days. Then, they rode in an airplane with stops in eleven different countries. They saw a lot of things, met many foreigners. Bought many presents, and learned a lot of customs, different from our own in America. Now, they should be satisfied they live in the best country in the world. America. Frederick already knew that he did, and was satisfied to stay at home, at the farm, raising his cotton, only coming to Grand Saline, and to their gin, to pick up his family and bring them home. He might be wondering if all of them would return to Big Sandy, after being in this town, so different from his own. They were slower. Lived slower, simpler. Maybe not. If he had delivered his cotton closer to Big Sandy, he would have already been home again, sitting on his porch, drinking a tall glass of sweet tea, by this time of day.

P.J. told his Daddy he was not known here, in Grand Saline as Junior Snow. His friends called him 'P.J.' He had written home that information on the very day of his name-change. His daddy congratulated him on making so many new friends.

"And they all brought presents, you say?" he said. "I guess your best one is that rug. You said it was a 'magic carpet' rug? "

P.J. had an enraptured look on his face. It was, indeed, his best present.

"S'pose to take you where you want to go, just by saying 'Gitty up go'. Is that right?" He kept on teasing his son.

"Going to take you to Arabia? To India? Maybe they should have just sent you an Aladdin's lamp; rub it and it would zap you there and back."

"Daddy, that is a good idea. But then I wouldn't get to see all there is to be seen, flying through the air on a magic carpet ride."

"I'll bet your uncle and aunt wish they could zap themselves here about this time. All that foreign business gets old after a while. But then, what do I know? I've never left the state of Texas."

Folks were throwing horseshoes. Playing the game to pass the time, while waiting to have their cotton ginned and weighed. Some were playing cards. All were eating and drinking and talking...meeting up with neighbors and making new friends. Offering new farm ideas, showing off new equipment. Frederick only wanted to get his cotton ginned and weighted, get the money for it, pick up his family from the Snow Hotel and take them home. Along with a nice bundle of cash promised by his brother, as payment for their babysitting the Snow Hotel. Frederick took out his pocket watch and checked the time. Would the First State Bank close their doors before he got his cotton ginned?

It was his time. They unloaded the cotton sacks. The boys came with their eighteen-inch suction pipe that worked up and down and back and forth to get the last bit of cotton out of the truck bed.

"Oh, let me do it. Please.", begged P.J. They let him.

Like a vacuum it would suck it straight up and out, right into the feed hooper or cage of the gin. That was already in motion. The rollers were coming down, working like a giant comb. Getting out all the burs, stems, hulls, sticks, and dirt. Cleaning the fiber. Half the cotton is seed that falls through the cracks and into a drop-pan to give back to the farmer to plant next season, or the company buys them. They make good feed for cows to eat. The roller brushes clean the cotton fiber until it is white as snow. Old Eli Whitney, one hundred and forty-five years earlier, knew what it took to clean up the cotton with his invention, his 'cotton engine'. People shortened that to 'cotton gin'. Still the same original design, housing is taller, two stories, to accommodate the 'crusher' or 'presser', that drops down hard, on the cotton bats, as many as seven times, pressing one layer on top of another, tightly, forming it into one size, that of a bale. The finished product will be weighed in at three hundred to five hundred pounds. Once that is done, it is 'payday' for the cotton farmer. It is weighed before they wrap it with jute and tie it with metal straps. It is then ready to load into trucks or onto the train that takes it away. In the case of Grand Saline, the train tracks run alongside the gin. The Texas & Pacific railway will haul it to Dallas and from there, to buyers from all over the world.

Frederick Snow told his son, "You can bet they'll get more than they pay us. We just plant the cotton, raise the cotton, pick the cotton, and haul it in. But they're the ones who have the cotton gin. And the buyers. They need us and we need them."

Today he would get eight dollars and sixty cents a pound. Tomorrow it might be more, or it might be less. During the depression it went down to twenty-seven cents. He would be happy to get his ticket to take to the paymaster. And be on his way. He would keep his seeds.

"Daddy, your cotton is the best there is."

"I know it.", Frederick said.

"I learned something I'll bet you don't know.", the boy said. "They make pink and blue cotton."

"Who's 'they'?

"Well, I mean God makes pink and blue cotton. It grows those colors in some places of the world."

Frederick said that if his ever came out pink or blue, he'd let him know.

"Daddy, can't I stay here a little bit longer? I hate to leave all my friends."

Frederick was sad but not angry. He loved his son and wanted him to be happy.

"Don't you miss your mama, and your little brothers? They miss you."

"I do, of course, but I can see them a little later. It's so fun living in town instead of in the country. They've always got something going on."

"Son, all the people who have made that happen for you, will be going home with you. Did you think about that?"

"But Daddy...", he started.

"Fred Snow, get down off that truck. The drivers are coming to take them back to Big Sandy... empty. Come on. I've heard enough of this nonsense. You're going home when I go. When we all go. And I hope all of us do go. Marilyn's letters hint she's gone and got her a husband picked out. I hope not. I hope we all go back home where we belong." He was just plain tired.

"Daddy, you called me 'Fred'. You never called me that before. You always called me Junior."

"I never called you 'Punjab' either, or P.J. I never called you a lot of things. But now you're thirteen years old. You're not a little boy anymore, Fred. You're a man at thirteen years old. The Bible says so. Now get down from there."

"Yes Sir."

"You're leaving lot of that kid stuff here, in Grand Saline, the turban with the tassel, the colored belt like girls wear, the white clothes..."

"Like Amm wears..." the boy reminded his daddy.

"Don't you talk back to me, Son. Or I'll make you leave that magic carpet here too."

"You're letting me take that with me?"

"If you'll use it to walk on, instead of ride on." He patted his boy's head that still was covered with the white turban with its jeweled tassel.

"Let's go blow out those thirteen candles now, Son. You reckon there's ice cream that goes with that cake?"

"If Ms. Bertha has anything to say about it. She's got it ready and waiting at the table in her café."

"You like her, do you?"

"Yeah. I mean Yes. Sir."

Ms. Bertha was waving a telegram in the air when they arrived at the 'Rayborne Café.

"Cecil and Miller Malone came in person to deliver this from their Western Union down at the M&M hotel.", she said.

Entering the door came Marilyn, Zasu and Amm, ready for birthday cake.

"What's that, Daddy?" He was reading the telegram.

"It's from your Uncle William. He's wanting you to stay an extra two weeks, while he takes his wife on a side trip to Switzerland. Because he wouldn't take her to Austria and Germany, where she wanted to go in the first place. She's wanting to see at least one of those three mountains. And Switzerland is neutral. It's safe. He's sweetened the pot for letting you stay. He's offered me the gold coin your grandfather got for his cotton when he took it to Louisiana that time. Years ago. The one you found under his buffet chest, Fred."

"The credenza.", said Marilyn. What are you going to do, Daddy?"

"Tell those Malone boys to send him an answer in one of their fancy telegrams. Tell him no thanks. We're going home."

That night P.J. and Deane took a ride on the magic carpet. She put her arms around his waist as he took hold of the two tassels on the front corners, to guide their way. The back two tassels were swinging their red, pink, yellow and green jewels attached to the colored rug at the end of each corner. They were free to follow the wind.

Five miles, they flew, taking a bare second to deposit them at the bottom of the 750 ft. elevator where they gazed at the vast salt walls, and open- door caverns, all God-made, of pure crystallized white salt. The tops were a hundred foot tall. The walls equally wide. The bottom was endless. All sparkled from the electric light bulbs that were strung from here to there. They had caught the wind that drove the magic carpet and swung back and forth, lighting the path it would most certainly take.

"Are you ready, Annie?", Punjab asked the little orphan girl. She shook her head yes, her orangish hair bouncing in anticipation for the experience of a lifetime.

"Gitty up Go.", ordered Punjab.

They took off, following the blinking lights. They flew forward, swerving just in time to miss a direct hit against the solid salt wall that had been carved out by sticks of dynamite set earlier. The smell of carbon lingered. They grazed the wall, without touching it and went down into a nosedive, coming back up like a rocket on fire, and flipping over to settle into flying saucer position. They would slow motion it now, through the thirty miles of halls made for the trucks, and jeeps and machines. They had been dismantled piece by piece, before being taken down, and put back together again at the bottom of the wooden elevator that ran by pullies lifting and lowering, people on one side, and tubs carrying up salt on the other. The vehicles would drive those roads carved out of the salt dome.

   Pillars of salt were left to secure ceilings. Miners, wearing I.D tags also wore their helmets, steel-toed shoes, and oxygen tanks, carrying their flashlights and lanterns. They would drive their loads of chunked salt to the nearest crusher. They were in motion now and the snow-like particles of salt flew through the air, like electric sparks.

   The magic carpet took the thirty miles in less than a second. The caverns beckoned and Punjab would show them to Annie, or rather Deane Dunne, in movie sequence. One cavern, two caverns, three caverns and 'zip' they were gone through those caves, leaving their shadows dancing on the walls inside, from the lights flickering on and off from light globes strung, and dancing themselves, from the motion of the wind that drove the magic carpet forward and onward.

  They hovered, for one last look at the inside of the Grand Saline Morton Salt mine. Off. Gone again. They shot up and out. There was the taste of salt in Annie's mouth as she sucked in the wetness of it in the air that she breathed. In fact, she was breathless, with the beauty of the salt mine they were now leaving, as if there were not 750 feet separating the mine from earth's surface. There were only stars to see now, bright and white, like the salt sprinkling Annie's hair, like the little girl on the box of Morton Salt was spilling hers. The little girl on the magic carpet shook her hair in wonderment, not daring to turn loose of Punjab.

They would follow the stars forming the milky way, lighting their pathway to their next adventure.

The magic carpet would ride the Arabian Seas. Punjab wanted to show Annie all he had heard about, from Daddy Warbucks about that magic land, sky, and sea.

CHAPTER 22

The magic carpet is green silk, and yellow to blend with all the colors of the Arabian sunset. From the golden-brown sand, yellow from the sun, there are layers of white hugging the earth, yet streaking across the sky's beginning, then uneven layers of pink, orange and red to burned beet red, then blue-black, like the water, and finally, at the top, sky blue. The moon showers its gold over all of it so that Punjab and Annie can see those wonders of nature.

The sea is salty because few lakes flow into it. It serves as playground for leaping dolphins and flying fish that look silver. Like the silver threads that blend with the gold of the magic carpet, on green silk. So is the sea, like green-black-gold-silver, rolling in waves, traveling nowhere. Traveling everywhere.

From the Punjab region in northern Pakistan, from the foothills of the stone range mountains, there is crystalized halite, mineral salt. There are mines of it; rock salt mines. There are caves and caverns, with small ponds and canals and even lakes. The walls are pink to red, along with yellow. This is not like the pure white in the salt mines of the United States. It is not used to sprinkle on food, though would do no harm. Pretty pink, it can accentuate food. Thought to give healing powers, that remains to be seen. Some believe it does. Most certainly the boy and girl riding the magic carpet would believe it to be so.

Mumbai, Maharashtra, Pakistan.

"This is it.", said Punjab. "This is the icing on the top of the cake."

The magic carpet hovers over 'Queen's Necklace'. Named that because of its C shape, the yellow lights come on at sunset, to illuminate the promenade on the beach. With the curve and shape, and the yellow lights, the boulevard looks like a dazzling Queen's necklace.

The beach that was tan, then brown, is golden now, the sea purple and dark blue. It will be black after sundown. The water is lapping, breaking, crashing as the tide comes in, curling with froth and seafoam, as the water is ebbing away, back into the sea. The sound is lovely, as she is, Marilyn, in her white dress. She is slightly chilled and there is Neely Berry to wrap his arms around her. And she is warmed.

Annie sees them first. On the Juhu beach.

'What is that on her head?"

"It's the crown of the Statue of Liberty. Does that mean she wants to go home? Shall we pick them up?", asks Punjab.

"No. They have their own dream. This one is mine." said Annie.

"Oh look. There are Amm and Zasu, See them? They are quite alone on the beach except for one glorious white horse."

"He rides. She walks. Wait. He is going to lift her up onto the white horse. Her arms encircle his waist, like I am encircling yours on this magic carpet.", says Annie.

She told Punjab, "They may want to stay here forever. You said this is their ancestral home. Maybe they don't want to go back to America."

Punjab said, "They wanted to see it. Like we have. But they must go home now. And so must we." And on a dime, the magic carpet turned westward. Off they went. In less than two minutes Punjab and Annie were home. And Deane Dunne opened her eyes. She rubbed them and blinked.

"P.J. Let me tell you what happened...".

She threw off the covers. Then remembered they had said goodbye yesterday. She wondered if he had the same dream. Of white salt mines in Texas, pink salt caves and caverns in the Himalayas, Arabian seas at sunset, and beaches with white horses and queen's necklaces. And best of all, of her, hanging on to Punjab, seeing all of it together, on a magnificent magic carpet ride.

She went back to sleep, then, perhaps to dream it all over again.

The End

Made in the USA
Monee, IL
08 November 2021